For Bobby & Faye
– Three little squeezes –

Prologue

Glory, 1927 – When the Dust Settles

"I think I know what it means now," Glory told her green ragdoll, stitched by her own hand and now stuffed feet-first up her long sleeve. Balancing on her tiptoes on her mother's hand-painted stool, Glory peered into the top shelf of her parents' wardrobe. She slid out the keepsakes box and balanced it carefully along her wooden hand.

"*When the dust settles*," she said with a voice way older than her eleven years. "That's what they kept telling me, so they did. From the second Mama was gone, they said things would be better when the dust settles."

1

Glory jumped down from the stool with such a thump from her leather boots it caused her big sister to yell something from the kitchen below. She kicked her own heel for being so noisy and rolled her eyes to the heavens. "It's nothing, Dee-Dee! I'm perfectly fine. Tripped, so I did."

Laying the box on the bed, Glory twisted her arm around so that the ragdoll's face looked down upon its dusty lid. "Well, Doll, do you think the dust *has* finally settled?" She took a deep breath in through her nose and sneezed. "I can do it..." she said as she pulled the ragdoll from her sleeve. "I can find a proper job, so I can – like a proper grown-up so I can put some pennies in Dee-Dee's rent tin. It's not fair she should be baking half the night to keep us in this house, you know." If the ragdoll had eyes, they'd have noticed a rare glint of fear in Glory's, for losing their mother and father to fever within weeks of each other was hard enough without the fear of losing their home too. "Bad luck comes in threes and that's a fact, so I got to do my bit," Glory gulped.

She lifted the lid. The box wasn't very full but everything in it was brimming with memories of her mother. She slowly swirled her wooden hand around its contents and snagged a pair of silk stockings with the tiny hook that protruded from the tip of her wooden forefinger. She fished them out and held them up before her.

"They'll do, for a start," she said. "They'll have me looking as old as Dee-Dee – sixteen at least." Although finding paid work wasn't unheard of for an eleven-year-old, she was smart enough to know that proper jobs were only open to teenagers who'd finished school, and mostly boys at that. Of course, she'd never let *not* being a boy stand in her way and, with the help of her mother's things, she'd surely give any teenager a run for their money. But there was little she could do about finishing school; despite doing well in all her subjects, the stuffy headmistress reckoned the school's efforts would be wasted on a girl with no future, as they saw it.

"They expelled me, you know. Because of this!" Glory held up her wooden hand and shook it hard. "Stupid hand. Stupid headmistress," she muttered and took a sidelong glance at her ragdoll. "*What?*" She could have sworn it questioned her with its button eyes. She bit the inside of her mouth until it hurt – had she kept it shut rather than shout back

3

all those words at the headmistress maybe she'd be learning algebra right this minute. But it wasn't her fault that she found it hard to keep her feelings, not to mention her words, to herself. Regardless, she had the right to a proper career, didn't she? A career in a fancy emporium doing what she loved best: designing jewellery.

She considered her mother's red lipstick, twisting it up before her, and noticed how it was perfectly formed to fit only her mother's kiss. She carefully placed it back into the box and, instead, stuffed a ruby red cloche hat under her arm. She swung the stockings over her shoulder, wrapped a string of beads around her neck and, from beneath the bed, pinched the heels of two laced-up grey and ivory boots.

Several minutes later, wearing her mother's best, she confidently strode to the mirror. Picturing a grand shop door before her, she knocked on the mirror's glass and pouted her lips just like the French ladies she'd seen outside the Fitzroy Hotel.

In her best grown-up voice, she addressed her reflection, "Good afternoon. Your jewellery emporium is looking rather splendid today. May I interest you in my designs?"

She just might get away with it; putting on a grown-up voice came naturally now that she spent most of her days without as much as a word to anyone her age. She patted down her dull, blue dress and made plans to accidentally borrow one of her sister's.

"I can do it," she said, again. She might actually land herself a job to keep the landlord at bay. Leaning forward, she squinted at her own eyes through the dusty mirror. "And who knows, Gloria Bobbin, if you keep your trap shut, one day you might even own an emporium of your very own." She knew too well that missing a hand meant being considered by some as hopeless, but one thing was for sure: she was a million miles from dreamless.

She bunched up the hat in her fist, ready to wipe the layer of dust from the mirror, but stalled. "Maybe I'll let the dust settle a little bit longer," she whispered, winked at herself and, for luck, crossed her fingers as tight as they would go.

Inthington Town of Old

– 2nd January 1864 –

A long, long time ago in a place called Inthington, where streets were made of cobble and the sky of black smoke, hardworking folk in horse-drawn carriages made their way to the fabric and button factories by a five-arched bridge. And there begins the story of a young mudlark: a boy who digs up long-lost, forgotten things from the muddy foreshore of the River Notion. *Treasures*, he named them – and his name was Needle.

Chapter One

Needle's longest nail was on his little finger – carefully nibbled into a point and perfect for rescuing. He reached down to the mud, faced his palm skyward and hooked the hidden treasure in one swift move.

SCH-M-OCK!

It was a slow sound and, if Needle tried to make it, he had to pop his lips open once he had done the *m* bit. It made a kind of sucking noise and Needle reckoned if it had a colour, it would be purple. That's what he always heard when he wiggled things free from the soggy mud.

"Fine work, Magpie. It be a ring, of sorts." Needle spat on it and rubbed it gently against the leather strap of his satchel. "*Gold*. It twists around twice on top, see?" He held it up close to Magpie's beak as she tiptoed around him. "And I be having you know it has four claws that once held a fancy gem." He placed it in the palm of his hand.

A painful shock of cold hit where the muddy treasure lay. He closed his eyes and waited to hear its story; somewhere inside, perhaps in the beat of his heart, he could feel it stirring. He stuck out his chest, stretched his neck high and put his free hand against the crook of his back.

"Easy, this one, Magpie. I see three girls paddling by the river's edge on a hot day acting like they be doing something they should not." He sneaked a peek at his audience of one and his lips stretched wide into a proud smile. "They be throwing pebbles trying to down bread that was thrown for the gulls and the girl dressed in blue threw a good one but the darned ring flew off with it. She didn't even know it was gone. It had a ruby stone in it one time and I be thinking she stole it from her aunt – a nasty old thing by the sounds of it. I be telling you more if the ruby were still in it." He opened his eyes, threw the ring in the air and caught it again. "Happened forty-odd years ago, at least."

To thank his bird for finding it, Needle stretched a worm from a tuft of frosty grass, taking care not to break it, and offered it whole. "Da didn't name you Magpie for nothing, you know. You might be a crow but you be putting real magpies to shame. They find shiny things but you're able to see shiny treasures even when they be covered in mud. The best treasure hunter in Inthington." He studied his crow. Were her cheeks blooming red beneath her feathers? Probably. If only he could find a way to hide his tell-tale cheeks too.

He scraped mud from the ring's band and held it high, allowing the sharp winter sun to bounce off its gold. "Mam'll be happy. Soon as I put glass in it, this ring be worth a pot of proper beef stew. And with Da being away, there might be some in it for you too, Magpie."

The treasure fit his forefinger best and, as the black hum of waking factories filled the air, his satchel was soon filled with more: half a dozen pieces of fine china, some copper wire, two bent coins, a belt buckle and a rose-shaped button – each with their own river-swept story.

They turned around when they reached the old

bakery that overlooked the River Notion to the right and where the walls of the town jail towered over to the left. Beyond that point was kept for warmer days; the tall walls cast shadows across the foreshore, so, on a frosty day, the hidden treasures were just too hard to dig. At least, that's what Needle might say if anyone should ask. To tell the truth, with Da no longer by his side, those bakery thugs were likely to hammer him with thrown bread – the burnt chunks that hurt.

Don't fight back for you might hurt the one bit of good in them, Needle's mother would warn.

But, if you're sure there's none in them, give as good as you get, his father would add.

As Needle listed the morning's bounty of river-swept treasure out loud, he thumb-twisted the gold ring around his finger, one full turn for each find. Along with the ring, there would be plenty in his satchel to bend, etch and sculpt into something his mother might sell on her market stall, but his eyes never left the ground.

Needle dropped to his haunches. Like a curious seal's head, a circle of glass with a blackened cork poked out of the mud. "Have you a story to tell?"

Needle asked the bottle's neck as he nudged it side to side. He bunched his coat sleeve around his hand should the old glass shatter and pulled. With a sch-m-ock came its reply.

"There be a letter in this bottle!" Needle yelled to his crow as she hopped along the edge where the pebbles met moss and grass. She was hunting for the shiniest of iridescent beetles.

Without rising, Needle tested the bottle's story, holding the muddy glass in the palm of his hand. He listened for a moment but soon opened his eyes. "It be about a boy, Magpie, maybe older than me. I think he poured his heart into this bottle," Needle said as he rubbed its surface clean with his thumbs. "It be his promise in here – his promise to bring his brother home with some secret plan." For comfort, Needle pulled himself up onto the embankment wall and sat down. He stared at the bottle, watching how the river sparkled through it.

"That letter inside might be telling me more." He pulled at the cork with his teeth; just maybe that secret plan inside would tell him how to bring Da home too.

He fished the letter out and, unable to read its

words, he held it in his palm, closed his eyes and waited.

Deep inside the story, the boy's secret plan began to unfold. Needle's own hope was rising when, along with the glass bottle, the story smashed to pieces on the foreshore; a cold hand had wrapped itself around Needle's jaw. He was pulled from the wall and slammed hard onto the flat of his back.

With air punched from his lungs, Needle opened his mouth to scream, to negotiate, to reason with, to say something, *anything*, but nothing came. Three thugs, full of fury and smelling of hot ovens, were pulling at Needle's chapped lips, yelling that the cat had his tongue. He saw flashes of Magpie's frantic wings between them as they tugged his leather boots from his feet and threw them deep into the River Notion. One of them, huge and long-armed, pulled his new ring – his planned pot of stew – from his finger.

As quickly as they'd arrived, they left, laughing and leaving Needle a crumpled heap on the road. He staggered to his feet and clambered back down to the foreshore. Magpie remained on the embankment wall, her head cocked to one side.

"Couldn't say nothing to stop them," Needle said, head and heart down. Why couldn't he just say something when spoken to? With his father gone, words just stuck in his throat.

They were right: the cat *had* gotten his tongue.

He squeezed and released his bare toes on the frosty pebbles. "Eleven," he said bunching his fists under his armpits, no longer able to count on his fingers the number of times such a horrid thing had happened. "Eleven times since Da left." He glanced at his crow – her angles were all wrong: stiff wings and claws tense, like she was standing on egg-shells.

"I be all right."

Magpie quietly deposited a gift of several wrigglers in Needle's palm.

Needle put them in his silver beetle box. "That'll be eight. That should do it," he said, the shake in his voice fading. As he slid the box into his satchel, a sharp pain shot up his leg.

"OUCH!" He grabbed his ankle and hopped in a circle, only stopping when Magpie cocked her head to the side again.

"No! I am NOT good! Blasted thing stabbed me, so it did," cried Needle. "I must be cut to bits. And wait till I get it in the neck from Mam," he added, picturing her waving her finger at his bootless feet. He threw his satchel down on the frozen mud and sat on it, not caring about its fragile contents. Certain there would be blood, he ripped a strip of grey cotton from the bottom of his shirt and folded his leg so the sole of his foot was propped up by his left thigh. With one wingbeat, Magpie balanced on Needle's knee.

"Well there be a thing, Magpie. Look at that," he whispered. He scrubbed his foot with the cotton. "Not a scratch!"

But skin began to rise on the ball of his thick-skinned foot. Magpie rested her chin on Needle's arm, hug-like.

"It be a blister."

Needle scrambled onto all fours with Magpie on his shoulder, searching the floor of frozen mud and pebbles before them.

He saw it first.

A small triangle of ripped metal had come up to the mud's surface for a gulp of air. Heaven knows how long it had been there, smothered and hidden beneath the plodding gulls and regular tides. This find was special. Needle touched it gently with his forefinger and winced. He sucked his fingertip despite the dirt, quickly pointed at the triangle and warned his crow with the palm of his other hand to stay away.

It was so darned hot.

❖

To think!

To think twelve years he'd been alive and such a thing as hot treasure existed without him ever knowing! He scooped the shard of metal out with stones, squinted at its etched letters and placed it on the strip of shirt cotton. He bunched it like a bag and held it up high. Was it *rare*? As rare as the treasures Da would bring home? *They* were so rare that a wipe of Da's thumb and they'd be ready to sell on Mam's stall – no tweaking or crafting at all. But this? *Hot* treasure?

Needle scanned the pebbles and mud around his feet for more, turning around slowly, searching in ever expanding circles. Something caught his eye: if he squinted, the foreshore was a vast sheet of grey frost. But dotted here and there – four in all – lay small circles of charming blue. The closest was to Needle's right, many yards away and only inches from the river's edge. He sped up with a limp, and stopped a yard shy of the blue patch. He sat down on his haunches.

"Magpie! Come see!"

Magpie flew to his side.

"Look at that. It be like someone ripped a piece of sky and dropped it to the ground."

Magpie, not fussed, walked up to the patch and circled it.

"Is there no poetry in you at all? Can't you see the beauty in it?"

It was water, free of ice and smooth as a mirror, with the cloudless blue sky above reflected within without a single flaw.

At the puddle's edge, Magpie stretched out her wings.

"Don't!"

Magpie did; she walked in. She was belly deep into the inches of water when she dipped her tail feathers and tossed her wings.

"It be hardly a day for having a wash, you fool!" Needle crawled forward and stuck his finger into the water.

"What?" He slapped both palms into the puddle. "It be warm! Yes! It has to be in there, Magpie – more hot treasure, melting all that ice!"

Needle scooped the water sideways until he revealed what he was expecting: another ragged piece of metal, larger this time with letters clear to the eye.

He hopped from one blue puddle to another, gathering the rest of his jigsaw, and soon the cotton bag bulged with five pieces of hot treasure. Holding his cotton-load straight out before him, he chased it, like a horse before a carrot, all the way back to Eyelet Bridge.

Clamping the cotton between his teeth, he checked for onlookers before urgently climbing up the stone face of the bridge between its first and second arch. Once he was over the black water of the River Notion, he figured the flat blocks of granite were slippery, so, with a whisper, he told his hands and feet to be careful. Just above the second arch, where the roadway joist jutted out above his head, he crawled into a gap not much wider than his body.

The gap, which could not be seen from above, was there because one block was missing. They didn't bother to put it there when they built the whole thing – if you make something and no one can see it, what's the point of that? So whoever didn't put the block there was a clever builder, just like Da. But Da was *so* clever that he was needed in a faraway place – *too far*. He was gone so long it hurt.

Needle slid the top half of his body into the gap and reached his hand back to his waist. He felt for the rope that was always tied around him, walked his fingers along it and grabbed the key at its end. Lying on his belly, he found the lock in the small driftwood door and inserted the key. It clunked beautifully in its usual ruby red way. He shoved the door open and wormed his way in.

He was through the gap, cotton bag of hot treasure in his hand with the words *Look, Da!* on his lips before he stood silently in Eyelet Bridge's hidden chamber, remembering that, in all his excitement, the one person he wanted to tell was not there.

Chapter Two

Inside the chamber over the second arch of Eyelet Bridge, Needle emptied the bag of cotton out onto a workbench. With tweezers, he turned the hot pieces until all sharp edges kissed and an incomplete rectangle took shape.

"You be one of them special signs – a *plaque*, I think you be called," Needle told it. "Only you be missing a square on the bottom." He grabbed an old hairpin washed up long ago that was without much of a story to tell and picked the last of the mud from the plaque's blocky letters.

"What took you?" asked Needle as Magpie flew in through her own small gap. "I reckon the treasure gods be sprinkling drops of good fortune on our heads today, Magpie."

Magpie looked up.

"Sure, where else could it come from? It be the only way to explain this hot treasure and all the fine treasures in our trove," said Needle as he waved his hand towards the tins and wooden boxes filled with scraps of metal, decorated buttons and hand-painted pieces of fine china. He nodded towards glass jars filled with bits of broken jewellery, sparkling sea-glass that looked like gems and mysterious, pretty things he had yet to name.

Not all were Needle's finds, of course – his father built this place to store *both* their treasures; he'd transformed the empty chamber over the second arch

into a workshop, complete with shelves, a workbench and a nest for Magpie: a thick wooden shelf, carved with a slight hollow and filled with washed-up fishing rope and twigs. This trove was where he taught Needle how to listen to treasures' stories, and this was where they tinkered by candlelight to transform long forgotten things into treasures to sell at the market.

Magpie released a large chunk of scone from her beak and chirped, chick-like.

"You went to the bakery? Did they throw stones?" Needle urgently asked, dropping the hairpin and scanning his crow's wings for damage. He counted her toes. When Magpie purred, Needle, suddenly starved, reached in for the scone. "Thanks." Strangely, it still held heat as though fresh from the oven but, to be sure, Needle checked it first for green mould. He bit into its corner. His teeth sank deep into the crumbly golden crust and then the beauty of it hit.

So spongy! So sweet and so tasty, like never before.

When he was done he looked Magpie in the eye. "Where did you find that?" It was hardly made by the hands of a bakery thug.

Magpie stretched her wings wide, fanning warm air towards him.

Without listening to her, Needle blew crumbs from the shards. "What do you reckon it says, Magpie?" he asked and felt a growing shiver, almost a shake, deep inside his belly. "Where to find the King's gold? Or one of them potion recipes?"

Magpie croaked.

"Or maybe them letters be saying you're the best crow in town." He gently folded Magpie's wings back to her sides and held her in his cupped hands. "I can get Mam to read it." He felt Magpie's urge to go. "But not now, eh?" He needed to make something special for Mam's market stall – how could he forget the colour of her voice when the landlord knocked on the door? "I have ideas for a candlestick with 1864 on it. Good, you think?"

Needle placed his crow down and turned his attention to the scattering of unfinished Christmas decorations to his right. Made of every kind of river treasure, they were skilfully glued, welded and stitched together into delicate yet hardy designs. He gathered them up, hanging a few on each finger. He posed like a tree for a moment before placing them in an empty wooden box.

"They be needing a glass bead or a twist of copper

but we can keep them for next year." He pulled out a metal tray from the side of the workbench and used it as a lid for the wooden box. With the hot shards on top, maybe the heat would spread across the tray and keep his fingers warm.

"Here," he said as he removed his silver beetle box from his satchel's pocket. Eight sleepy beetles, hunted earlier by Magpie, lay within. He pulled one out and watched its legs stretch. Kissing it first, he said sorry and plucked off its wings. "You can start on them, just save me the wings."

As Magpie enjoyed her breakfast, Needle prepared for work. As was always the routine, he pulled at the string around his neck until the smooth, oval stone it carried squeezed past his collar. He held the stone between his fingers and peered through the perfect hole in its centre. He treasured his stone, it being one of the first things he and Da found together. *A rare hag stone*, Da called it.

"Listen to my breath, Magpie. It does be slowing down when I look through this hole. Da says it be like time slowing down and he's right." As Needle squinted, he felt his worries shift. The worry for his father, soothed. The twist in his stomach each time he tried to speak up, loosened. The lump in his throat each time his mother said sorry for serving the same food, melted. In his mind, he was in another world – a *better* world. He placed his stone back through his collar, took a deep breath and began his work.

Several hours had passed by the time Needle pulled a scrap of paper from his shirt pocket and studied the digits for the year 1864 that his mother had written down. He thumb-rubbed the new candlestick's handle – a twisted fork, prongs splayed and topped with sea-glass for added joy – and decided where best to etch. For courage, he wished his nervous fingers good luck.

Magpie, hungry again, began to fuss.

"Maybe you could find more of them fancy scones." It sounded more like an instruction than a suggestion, and Needle regretted that. "Mam would love some," he added with an apologetic smile.

Before she left, Magpie answered in her way; turning her head to the side so she could see all of Needle with one eye, she stretched out one leg and tucked it back up under her belly. Needle took that as meaning *all was good.*

It was dark when Needle arrived home. He pushed open the door and a blast of warm air and the smell of something delicious hit. He sneaked over to the kitchen table that sat in the centre of the small room. His mother stood at the stove with her back turned and, bar a twitch, she didn't move.

Had she heard him? Probably – his unblistered foot had smacked the stone floor with every limped step – but she was playing along, so he quietly placed his candlestick on the table. Feeling beneath the table's top, he stuck his finger into a small hole that once housed a wooden handle and he levered out the drawer. He found a candle, placed it and lit its wick. Light bounced off the candlestick's cut-glass beads and shimmering beetle-wings. Golden specks dotted the white-washed walls.

"Now?"

"Now, Mam."

She wiped her hands on a cloth, flicked hair away from her face and turned.

"Magic, my love!"

Needle gently spun the candlestick clockwise and

she spun too – she floated gracefully around and around, whistling Needle's favourite yellow tune, danced her way to the door and closed it.

"It be missing one beetle-wing – Magpie left me short; she nicked number sixteen," he grumbled.

"But fifteen looks much better!" She waited for his agreement, smiled when it came and pointed at his masterpiece. "That will fetch a fair price, it's beautiful. Well done," she said, and she meant it, "but don't begin just yet." She returned to the stove, filled two bowls with steaming soup and carried them to the table. Pulling two spoons from a glass jar, she handed Needle his favourite – a short handled, finely engraved river find that held a story of a party and a delicious thing called jelly.

"I'm ready," she said and sat opposite Needle, the candle flickering between them.

And so, he began. He touched each part of the candlestick with the palm of his hand and waited for the shock of cold to hit. He shared story after story: the six-fingered murderer with silver rings so heavy they stretched his arms and hunched his back; the sewer rat, proudly lining up its collection of stolen keys; the jealous wigmaker and her wig of pure gold thread; and the spider amulet, worn around the neck, that blessed or cursed its wearer with an irresistible urge to dance. A bookful of stories written into every bead and every twist of metal. For a boy who could never find words from a sea of letters on a page, he was a storyteller who could read his treasures to perfection.

The fire in the stove had flattened by the time they were done. His mother placed her hands around the candlestick and blew out the candle. "You've made a treasure, Needle, and now each part's story has been told, this candlestick's own story begins right this very second. It's lovely – your best yet." She ruffled his hair and pushed back her chair. Rather than rise, she slapped her thigh. "Now show me your foot. I heard you limp." Her voice was suddenly red. "Your boots?"

"Thrown to the gulls, Mam." Needle slowly raised his foot and rested it on her leg. "Good thing they didn't throw my bag too?" he added, in the hope she would see the bright side he'd dug deep to find.

Her tight lips softened and so too did her voice. "Oh, Needle. Those bakers again? The Selvage brothers?"

There was no need to answer. Instead, he wriggled his toes and awaited her reaction.

She stared down at the wound, gently holding his toes to keep them still. Using her thumb, she wiped the day's gathering of dried mud to the right and softly blew it away. Not the touch but the warmth of her breath made Needle flinch.

"How did this happen?"

"Me and Magpie were, you know, *schmocking*," he said and made eye-contact to check if she was annoyed by his choice of words; *it sounds rude*, she'd told him before, but how could the birth of his treasures be rude? "And sure there it was, stuck in the mud and out to get me." He pulled his satchel from the back of the chair and waved his hand above the warmth that spread from the bundle of grey shirt cotton. He quickly sat straighter to tuck his ripped shirt into his trousers and grimaced at his mother's stern eyes, filled with disapproval.

"I had no choice, Mam. I had to wrap them in something and I was out by the river with nothing else," he said and offered the satchel to her. "Careful now, they be hot."

"Hot?" Her voice grated – to Needle, it was orange:

31

afraid. Pulling back the layers of cotton, she pinched the sharp point of one metal shard.

"MAM!" cried Needle, wincing at the pain she must be feeling.

She hoisted the triangular shard out of its cotton bed and placed it in the palm of her hand. "Cold as ice, see?"

Needle made a grab for it.

"NO!" she yelled and pulled it away and placed it on the table. "It'll burn you."

"Huh?" Mam was not making sense and it was all confusing. Hot or cold, yes or no – simple answers. Why couldn't the world be made up of black or white, and not all the grey in between?

"It's… *complicated*," she offered, and rubbed his shin as she explained. "When you find things in the mud, how do they feel to you?"

Needle shrugged.

"*Think*. And don't be so afraid to make mistakes! Or of saying something that others don't agree with. Just say it! Your treasures – what do they feel like when you find them?"

"Dunno. Really cold, I think?" Needle sat up straighter; his answer was good. "They go icy, Mam, in my hand. The older the thing is, the colder it feels. So cold it hurts sometimes. But then I can see it all."

"That's the past you can see."

"You can see what happened to the treasure when you think real hard about it. You know who carried it in their pocket, like you be standing in their shoes. You are awake but it's like a dream, isn't it?"

"Well, as I've told you before, I wouldn't know, pet. That's your special thing. Like the way you hear things in colour. Aren't you lucky? Who wants to be just another grey pebble like all the rest? But best maybe to keep your special things to yourself," she added and patted his cheek. "*Unique.* That's what you are."

He couldn't recall being called such a shiny gold word before. "But anyone can be reading them treasures, you know? You just need to slow down and throw out all your thoughts" said Needle.

"*Clear your mind,* you mean. I wasn't able, last we tried."

Needle blushed. He'd picked the wrong words, *again.* And it was true about her trying to read treasures – she'd cupped Da's teacup in her hands the other night. What *were* those thoughts she couldn't throw out? "Da's a better teacher, Mam, he teached me and he'll teach you… Do you think it could be a bridge or a tower? A castle, Mam?" Whatever his father was building these days had to be most important. Why else would he not come home for Christmas?

"Perhaps."

Typical. He was guaranteed to get a one-word answer if he mentioned his father. Needle missed his father dearly since his mother said he'd travelled someplace else for work. He had a million questions he wanted to ask, most of them starting with *why*. But, for whatever reason, his mother's talking would shut down – every single time.

"But, this piece, Mam." He pointed to the hot shard. "I can't hold it to hear its story."

"Don't worry yourself about that." She slapped her hands to shake any dust and any further explanation away. "You need something for your foot." She stood up, whipped the dishcloth from her shoulder and levered up the hot handle of the steel barrel that sat above the stove. She dipped the dishcloth into the bubbling water and tore a narrow strip. Needle watched as she cleaned his foot and bandaged it up carefully. She reached over to the steel door to the left of the crackling embers and popped up the catch. A pair of warm woollen socks were waiting within and she pulled them up over his feet.

"Da's?" He said it again.

She turned her back to wipe her eyes. Needle gasped. *Tears?* They be only socks! But, maybe with Da long gone, they were a bit like treasure too.

Needle's mother took a deep breath, lifted the seat of the bench beside the front door and reached in for his father's old boots. "You'll wear these from now on." There was a blue tinge to her voice.

Needle stood up and slid his feet into the boots – easily done considering there was more than enough room to squeeze and release his toes inside. Turning his back to his mother, he discreetly wrapped the laces around several times before tucking them in and out of random eyelets. He studied the tangled mess at his feet. Anyone could hand him a bagful of river-swept things and he'd transform them into treasures, but tie boot strings with one of those fancy bows?

"Better?" he asked, hoping his attempts would cheer her up. When she smiled, he pointed to the hot shard. "So, why is this hot and not cold like the others? Is it treasure at all?"

"It *is* treasure, Needle. A fine one. But this piece is not an old treasure from the past…" She sat down and held her fingers to her lips as a tear broke loose from her eye and rolled down her cheek. "This treasure, Needle… this treasure is from the *future*."

The future? The thought of it bounced around his head but had nowhere to settle. He scanned her eyes, desperate to know more. "I found others – they've letters too."

She pulled her chair closer to the table.

"Your father, with Magpie's help, found a piece of that treasure too. I saw it with my own eyes and I saw what it did to him. The palm of his hand was scarred, possibly for life."

Needle gasped. A bandage on Da's hand not long before he disappeared – he remembered that. Mam wrapped it each evening, just as she had done to his foot.

"His hand was scarred, but so too was his mind. He thought of nothing else, day in, day out. He was fascinated by it – a hot square of metal, strangely etched with a date well into the future. And soon, he was on that foreshore seeking more. He was out there digging more than he should and, well, he didn't mean for it to happen, but his work suffered. That meant things got hard. *So hard*, Needle. For all of us." She blew her nose.

She was choosing her words and saying them with great care, making sure they were just the colour she wanted them to be. But, to Needle's ears, her words were so worried they were muddy.

"So he left to find work?"

"He just left and we need him back. For the food, for the clothes on our backs, for this place…" She raised her hands up in despair and cried something about their landlord before dropping her voice to a whisper. "But, most of all, Needle, it's the being *without* him. I miss him. I miss him. I *miss* him."

"When's he back, Mam? Where is he?"

She shook her head and dipped her eyes.

Needle held his breath. Did that mean she didn't know? Like a cold breeze, he could feel her worry surround him, itching to get into his head too.

"Mam? He's coming home?" he tried, again. He could see she was trying to speak, but it was like sadness or fear had bolted her throat shut – he knew exactly how that felt, trapped words screaming to

37

escape until they make your insides ache. But no words came and she made sure of that by covering her face with her hands.

Her voice was broken.

It was gone, *colourless*.

And it shocked him.

This was his fault – *he* made her speak of Da. *He* did that to her, not knowing of her worry, and he didn't know how to fix it. "I… I be sorry, Mam. Please." He jumped up, knocking the chair to the floor. Nervously bobbing from one foot to the other, he stepped closer to her. He took hold of her thumb, not sure what to do next. "Please, Mam." He jiggled her thumb and broke into a croaky song – one that she sang when things were good.

She wiped her face with the palms of her hands. "Let me see them, pet – your treasures."

Needle moved the candlestick to the side and emptied the shards onto the table. Without touching them, he directed her until all were in the correct position. She placed her palms on the table and read the future.

"Gosh, Needle."

"What?"

"In Memory of the Lost Souls who drowned in the Great Flood on the night of the 6th January, 1928 at Eyelet Bridge, Inthington," she read.

"That be sixty-four years after now!" shouted Needle.

His mother smiled, trusting his answer was right – the ability to read may have passed him by but counting was different. "And there's more: see these bits?" She ran her finger along the lines of smaller letters. "These are the names and addresses of the people who died. *Will* die. Fourteen names in all, I'm guessing. The bit that goes here held the last name." She rubbed the table where a square corner was missing. "I remember because that's the bit your father found. And it had a round stamp in the corner that was dated 1928. That's the part that really confused and excited your father. He was too curious as well, Needle." Her eyes grew glassy.

"He'll be back. You'll see," said Needle as he patted her on the back just the way his father would pat his when he promised his luck would change and he'd catch a fish. "Da is just busy building something. We be having a party that day, with cake and all, Mam. Oh, cake!"

He dug deep into his satchel and pulled out Magpie's cake, delivered to his lap before he left for home. He unfolded the paper in which he had wrapped it and held it towards his mother. It was a slice of yellow sponge and, now that he could see it more clearly, it had a shocking yellow top. Still warm, from the shards no doubt, he held it up high.

"Eat, Mam. It's cake, a gift from Magpie – fresh today." He broke off a piece with his muddy fingers and held it up to his mother who smiled and accepted it. He stuck the swoop of icing that covered his finger into his mouth and winced and flapped his hands, bird-style.

He had never tasted lemon before.

Chapter Three

"Mam's words have no colour, Magpie," said Needle as he sat in his trove, picking at Magpie's latest offering: a slice of warm, nutty bread. "She didn't tell me till now because she said my head wasn't ready to take her worry. I have to find Da – Mam needs him back." Needle looked at Magpie and wondered if he needed to add that *he* needed his father back too.

Magpie hopped up onto Needle's knee. He offered her a crumb – held it right up to her beak, but she gently tipped her tail off his lap. *New language.* What was she trying to say?

"Me too." Needle guessed, rightly or wrongly, that perhaps she was missing his father too. "Go stretch your wings. I need to make more bits for Mam to sell, maybe a decoration for them fancy doorknobs." Magpie obeyed and Needle sighed, attempting to get rid of his disappointment; he knew *what* he needed to do – find his father – but the *how* was not so obvious.

He leaned across the workbench and removed the metal tray from the wooden box where he'd stored his unfinished Christmas decorations; with the ground still frozen outside, perhaps, with a bit of tinkering, they'd do the job of cheering up the most serious of doorknobs. He reached his hand into the box and patted around, unable to see the contents for the box was deep and the sides were high. Anything would do, for starters. After pulling out a rogue hairpin, he stood and peered into the box. A ceramic square and just the one, almost complete decoration remained within. That was all! He shook from deep inside.

"THIEF! THIEF! WE'VE BEEN ROBBED! MAGPIE!" He threw his satchel over his shoulder, jumped up to the metal post above the door and swung his feet through the gap. Turning onto his belly, he slammed the driftwood door and, shaking, fired the key into the keyhole.

"Huh?" The door was always kept locked. Always. *"Magpie?"* he asked himself in disbelief. He ripped his knees off the rough stone as he shimmied out. Hugging the flat stones on the face of Eyelet Bridge, he twisted his body to the right and left, shielding his eyes from the glaring sun. He was in search of the thief: Magpie.

"Where you be? MAGPIE? I'll surely pluck every feather from your tail, you robbing—"

There was a plop and a splash to Needle's left and a tell-tale scone with red berries came up to the water's surface and bobbed along with the flow of the river. Needle's eye followed a straight line upwards until it met the neighbouring gap above Eyelet Bridge's third arch.

"DON'T YOU MOVE, YOU THIEF! Oh, you be in for a right slap now!" He climbed across the bridge's blocks, all the while directing each hand and foot to its planned destination. "Thought I wouldn't look in that box till next Christmas, eh? Well, you been found out and you be in for a hiding."

He spotted Magpie's head jutting out of the gap above the third arch and he lunged towards it. He hoisted himself up and dragged himself in. The gap's surface was not what he expected, it being smooth and curved at the edges, but now wasn't the time to ponder.

"Da told me about you and your thieving so I know all about how you met – swiping things right out of his hand…" Through the gap, he poked his head into an empty chamber, much like his trove. In the absence of a metal post out from which he could swing, he slumped down, hitting his head on the cold, damp floor.

Needle groaned. His forehead throbbed and his jaw ached. He knelt and opened his eyes. Blackness, the deepest kind, surrounded him only for a slice of light coming from the gap up high.

"Magpie?" he whispered, meaning to shout.

Magpie was gone and his head spun. Had he been knocked out? For how long? Dizzy thoughts flew around his head as his eyes adjusted and grey forms took shape around him. The space was similar in size to his own trove yet it was clear no man had made use of it. He pulled himself up to standing with weak knees and jelly arms. His boot snagged something –

a rope or string perhaps – and he jiggled his leg to free it. When he put his foot down, it didn't hit hard, cold rock.

Underfoot was soft, squishable, *uneven*.

"*Magpie?*"

Needle dropped to his knees. "No! NO!" he cried, his stomach retching with regret for allowing his voice to be so red when he'd chased his bird. Holding his breath, he felt blindly for what he did not want to see.

He made contact.

Urgently reading its shape with his fingers, he howled with relief. Whatever it was, it was not Magpie. As loud as his voice would allow, he swore never, ever to think ill of his crow again.

He held the damp thing up to the light.

"Could it be?" he asked. He turned it in his hands, feeling every bit of its surface. "Da's bag!" He knew it well! Green sacking stitched by Mam, with a three inch trim of leather – perfect for sitting on wet pebbles.

Needle crawled over to the far corner of the chamber where the strip of light crossed the darkness and met the floor. His hands trembled and his head throbbed as he tipped the contents of the bag out onto the floor: a chisel, a pocket-watch, a tin box filled with matches and a familiar, slim wooden box. Before his father left, that same box had confused Needle when he'd found it on the kitchen windowsill, for the lid was not hinged but slid out to the side. He'd wondered why his father had not passed the finds within to his mother to sell or, at least, to his son to transform them into something worthy. *For a rainy day*, was his father's explanation, but Needle knew by the way he caressed them, they must have been his favourites. With his father missing, Needle now let them become his favourites too.

One was a green glass marble from nearly ninety years ago. Needle placed it in the palm of his hand and let its story begin: for weeks it was abandoned in the coat hem of a nose-picking pickpocket before being hurled through the window of a poor family. It rolled to the foot of a boy. Such joy the marble brought! Together with four other boys in a sloping field on a scorching hot day, he dug a shallow pathway with his heels for their five marbles to roll down towards a brook. He cheered it along its journey to the water, but then it rolled off course to clang the curved handle of a buried golden chalice. As his eyes feasted in amazement on the chalice, hidden by a cruel and murderous bishop – now a skeleton somewhere – his marble rolled on to win the race. It was swept away by the current but little did he care.

Needle opened his eyes. The story felt so *real* this time – much more so than when he'd held it at home. He could still feel the warmth of the sun and the dusty earth tickled his nose. He sneezed and dropped the marble onto the floor of the chamber.

Feeling strangely overcome by heat, he looked along the strip of light that crossed the chamber. A dandelion seed with its umbrella of fluff, just like the ones he would blow apart to tell the time, floated down towards him and landed on his shoulder. *How odd!* A summer seed? He flicked it off. What on earth was it doing here? "It be winter," he told it as it disappeared into the darkness.

He sought out the marble and placed it back in the box between a delicate bone comb and a small wooden handle from the drawer beneath their kitchen table at home, wrapped neatly in cotton – a curious keepsake, but not as curious as the box's final offering: a medicine bottle, complete with a stopper, a well-worn label and an inch of green liquid. His mother caught him once pulling at the stopper with his teeth and she'd warned that the letters said it could kill you. But the bottle told Needle a different story: just a spoon full of that green liquid had made many a sick person better.

Needle packed his father's things into his own satchel and, checking for more, he patted his father's damp bag and slid his hand into its side-pocket.

Heat tipped his fingers.

He shook the bag and the silver clang of metal-on-stone echoed around the chamber.

"The missing piece," he whispered as he peered down at a hot, square-shaped metal shard. There were letters on it, as expected, and he saw the circular date stamp that his mother mentioned too.

"Wait till she sees this. And wait till she sees all these things," he said. "*Da's* things." His breath quickened, his heart raced. Such joy! He pictured her sheltering his father's things under her chin, smiling, swaying, singing. *A piece of Da.* But then he froze – a question grew: *Why* was the bag there? What did this mean? He felt that familiar pang in his belly, the one he always felt when he didn't know the answer to a question. *Would Mam know?*

Unwilling to rip more from his shirt, he tugged at his tangled bootlaces and kicked one boot off. He removed his sock, slid his hand into it and reached for the shard.

The thick wool offered just enough protection and it was then that an idea came to him – what if he could feel this shard's story, just like the other old treasures he'd found? He had never tried it for fear of getting burned, but it now sat in the palm of his hand, just hot enough to bear, on a layer of thick wool.

He closed his eyes and waited. The heat thickened and thickened and the shard's story began.

Quietly at first, like thoughts that float between awake and sleep.

With a wobble in this breath, he took great care of this story; like capturing a butterfly in the lightest finger-cage, he held it ever so delicately in his mind until it grew.

And grew.

And took flight.

The shock of cold in his palm spread and goosebumps rose on his arms. The sudden coldness of the air almost overwhelmed him. A whooshing blacker than black sound filled his ears, the ground beneath him shook, his breath raced, faster and faster. He gasped for air and felt his mouth and his eyes and his ears fill with icy cold water and he could not breathe. *Could not breathe.* He could not save himself. His arms flapped and he threw the shard with its terrifying story of flooding to the floor, and opened his eyes.

He swallowed a lungful of air so cold it stripped his throat. His head felt muddled and dizzy but, as he stared down at the shard, two things were clear: no soul should be lost to that god-forsaken flood. And, to be so sure of that, he needed his father to help him.

A pecking stirred him from his thoughts.

"Magpie!" He threw the shard and sock into his satchel, pulled the strap across his chest and grabbed his boot. "I be coming – wait there! I won't be cross with you, cross my heart!" With great effort, he scrambled up the chamber wall to peer through.

Needle stalled. He felt for the bump on his head – he must have hit the ground hard when he fell into the chamber, for the gap through which he'd entered was a clear, body-width hole. Now it was blocked by a wall of orange bricks. Fist-sized holes were dotted around the curved edges where the gap had been, pouring lines of light his way.

On the other side of the largest hole was a blinking eye.

"Magpie?"

His crow flew off.

Needle heaved himself up so that his hips balanced on the edge. He forced his hand into the toe of his boot and hit the brickwork again and again until chunks dropped down onto the River Notion on the other side. With dust and sweat in his eyes, he sucked in his stomach and dragged himself out.

As soon as his head poked out above the third arch of Eyelet Bridge, the wind whipped his face and vicious sleet forced him to blink and spit. Securing his boot's leather between his teeth, he splayed his hands to the side and looked down.

What he saw, he would never forget.

His belly flipped. His throat yelled. *Gone* were the tinkling waves as they gently stirred pebbles on the shore. *Ice* – vast, thick sheets of it, creaked and throbbed and heaved below him. *A frozen river*, the likes of which he had never seen before.

He pulled himself out, grabbing the icy road joist

above. His hands slipped. He fell down, landing feet first with his arms stretched out, beside his bird and his boot on the ice below.

He squinted through the storm of sleet, towards home – the first in a row of five white cottages on Broidery Quay.

Home was GONE, and it took Needle's breath with it. A gigantic grey building, with rows of steps and serious pillars, stood in its place.

Gone was the sweet smell of the bakery factory.

Gone was Inthington's brown sound of horse hooves and the factories' black hums.

Gone was everything he thought he ever understood.

He looked down: his bird, his boot – two familiar things. He scooped them both up, terrified and desperate to hold on to what was normal, only to drop them again. He grabbed two fistfuls of his hair and spun around. Eyelet Bridge, with its five arches and every familiar block of stone, stood before him. It was *right*, it was *normal* – it was *his* Eyelet Bridge. He spun again, to face the foreshore. Everything he saw was wrong: the stones in the embankment wall reached higher, two foot at least. The road above it was lined with unusual black poles, twisted and topped with lamps, and grown-up trees he'd never set eyes on before.

"GO BACK. GO BACK. GO *BACK!*" he screamed at himself. He grabbed his boot and clambered up to the gap over the third arch of Eyelet Bridge. Once inside, the blackness swallowed him up and he folded himself into a tiny ball in the corner. He sat, hugging his knees and his satchel tight, rocking back and forth. For what must have been hours, he ignored Magpie's manic attempts to make him move and focused on the strip of light that shone from the gap, highlighting a circle on the chamber floor. When the light finally climbed the wall and began to fade, he allowed himself ten attempts to climb out and glance at where home should be. Each and every time, it was gone. In the fading evening light, he looked down at the frozen river, scanning it for Magpie.

"Magpie?" he cried, his head jutting out of the gap. He yelled both her name and Mam's again and again in a wild roar of fear. Magpie swooped down and her wings clipped his face. She landed on the ice before him and stomped her feet as though urging a worm to rise up from below.

Needle climbed down. His breath quickened, like he had run a mile.

"Magpie, where are ..."

There was no point in asking where he was – he *knew* the answer: under the third arch of Eyelet Bridge on the River Notion in Inthington Town. Without doubt, it was not anyplace else. And that's when it dawned on him.

It was *not* another *place*.

It was another *time*.

Inthington Town

– 2nd January 1928 –

In a time somewhat closer to ours, stood the same Inthington Town but an entirely different world; people were doing their best to wash their memories clean of The Great War which had killed and wounded millions and haunted the minds of countless more. The fortunate ones enjoyed wild flapper parties and fast motorcars, and searched out fancy shops for fashionable things to wear. Elegant hats, silk shoes, rings and bangles – all that sparkled. And, in the middle of it all, was a young jeweller's apprentice called Glory.

Chapter Four

*T*HWACK! Glory's knuckles felt it before the sound even hit her ears.

"You're a good-for-nothing freak!" spat Mrs Quick. "*Look* at me when I address you." She cocked back today's chosen weapon – her oversized hairpin – and stabbed the desk with its sharp point. "What do you call *this*?" She pulled something out from behind her back and thrust it too close to Glory's eyes.

Glory backed up a bit and focussed on the piece of jewellery Mrs Quick held by her fingernails as though it were stinking dirt.

"Mrs Quick, that's my work from this morning." She sighed. "It's an oval brooch made with sapphire and aquamarine beads set in plenty of gold filigree. Just as you asked."

Mrs Quick shook it vigorously. Two glass beads dropped from their clasps and bounced across the desk. She snapped the pin off easily and held it beneath Glory's chin. "You forgot *spectacular*," she spat, the pin's point scratching at Glory's skin with each word. "I *demanded* spectacular and, when I say spectacular, I mean not just in design, but in *quality*." Mrs Quick fired the pin across the workshop, squeezing the brooch so hard it broke.

Without taking her eyes off Mrs Quick, Glory wiped a droplet of blood from her chin.

Mrs Quick hissed. "For generations the Frippery & Fandangle Emporium has been known for its quality and you, you impetuous runt, have no place here unless you pull yourself together. DO YOU HEAR ME?"

"I have ears – I *do* hear you," replied Glory, doing her best to suck in her sarcasm, not to mention her seething frustration. She stared at the lipstick that bled outwards like spiders' legs from Mrs Quick's wrinkled up lips and bit down hard on her own for fear that the words she *really* wanted to say would escape.

Mrs Quick bared her yellow teeth. She scooped

up her Jack Russell, tucking the stiff dog under one armpit. "Do *not* let me see anything less than spectacular quality or you'll serve the rest of your apprenticeship cleaning gutters."

Glory sighed. She so needed this job; the Frippery & Fandangle Emporium, though without doubt the best of its kind in Inthington, was last on her list of potential employers – Mrs Quick *did* have a reputation after all. But when all the other jewellers took one look at the young, one-handed girl before them and slammed their doors, she realised her last resort would have to do. It took an armful of the most exquisite drawings, along with what she concluded could only have been luck, to prove she was worthy of her apprenticeship. Without this opportunity, her homeless future quite likely *would* involve gutters. Glory clenched her fist.

A cold draught forced its way under the ruby velvet curtain, chilling the workshop, and the bells over the door of the shop signalled the arrival of another sequin and tassel-laden shopper.

"Keep your mug down," warned Mrs Quick before turning on her heel, announcing her 'do come-in's' in a higher than natural pitch. "Come now,

Maximus, we have a customer to whom we must attend."

"You're a *fake*," Glory mouthed and stuck out her tongue as soon as Mrs Quick had closed the curtain to return to the shimmering jewels and handcrafted riches of the shop floor. Pushing back her stool, she defiantly decided she more than deserved a break; it had not been much past six that morning when she'd dragged herself out of bed and walked the icy streets of Inthington, crossing Eyelet Bridge and on to the emporium. By the recent chimes of the grandfather clock that stood the other side of the curtain, she knew it was now well past twelve and, if she was to redo that brooch for Mrs Quick, she needed a lungful of fresh air and something for her stomach too.

With one eye on the curtain, her hand felt blindly for her beaded pouch bag, hidden beneath her apron and between the folds of her skirt. Her fingertips made contact with its beads. Forbidden and hidden beads, indeed; over the course of two months sitting at her desk, each bead had most definitely accidentally fallen onto her lap and down into her boots until it made its presence felt by sticking between her toes. At bedtime they were secretly stitched onto her handmade bag. All accidental of course, but kept hidden nonetheless.

Out of spite, she squeezed a random green bead through the bag's tassel-tied neck. "Serves her right, Doll, doesn't it?" she whispered to her favourite thing hidden deep inside: a hand-stitched ragdoll made entirely of green. She waited until she heard the jangle of Mrs Quick's keys being readied to open display cabinets before tiptoeing along the narrow corridor that lead to the back door.

She opened it, quiet as a mouse.

"Are you here?" Glory whispered into the small, damp yard. Her voice echoed gently against the stone walls and her breath surrounded her in a haze as she crept around the wrought iron table that sat in the centre.

"Come now, don't be a shy little thing," she added softly. She returned to the door and sat down on the cold step. Pulling her crocheted shawl close around her neck, she placed the beaded bag on her lap and began to detangle its knot of tassels. As the strings of gold beads flapped and rattled, so too did something in the far corner, just behind the dark ivy.

Glory reached into her bag, pulled out a sweet scone and tore off a corner. She tossed it across the pavestones just to the left of the table and whistled a gentle song.

"There you are. How have you been, little miss?" Glory watched the crow hop on two legs from the corner. It then strutted along, with its strong beak held high and feathers so black they were blue. It stopped just shy of the scone.

"You're looking fine today. I've brought you one of my sister's scones. She made them for my birthday. I'm twelve now, so I am, but don't tell Mrs Quick – she thinks I'm sixteen," she added proudly as she

tucked stubborn red curls behind her ears. "Try the scone, I think you'll find it's nice."

The crow eyed the spongy yellow meal. In one wingbeat it landed on the twisted metal of the garden chair. With claws clamped around the frosty wrought iron, more than once, it dipped its head down towards the scone and then up to face Glory.

"Don't be shy. It's even nicer than our usual bread. Try it or I dare say I shall name you Fusspot!"

The crow straightened itself up and stood tall like a black statue. It remained so for some time and stared deep into Glory's eyes.

Glory accepted its stare; she didn't dismiss it, fiddle or make idle chat. That moment felt beautiful. She had been feeding this crow since she began her apprenticeship, making her daily effort to befriend her feathered friend. And now, finally, they seemed to have made a special connection.

The cash register dinged.

"Have to run or terrier-face will have my guts for garters. She's a mean old bat, Fusspot. Never happy with anything I make." She felt her cheeks redden. If she was honest, it was *she* who was never happy with anything she made – bringing her designs to life, from a rather good sketch to a wearable piece of jewellery, was proving harder than she ever imagined. With her job threatened daily, she was helping her sister fill the rent tin by the skin of her teeth and her dream of one day owning her own emporium was fast becoming no more than a rough sketch itself; with every loose bead and fallen gem, it was fading fast.

"Go on, Fusspot. Take your dinner and I'll see you tomorrow." With one finger and thumb, Glory tied her bag and, as she leaned forward to rise from the step, the crow flew down from the chair, hopped over the large corner of scone and landed before Glory's laced-up leather boots.

It stooped and something small dropped from its beak. It grabbed the scone and flew up and out of the yard, disappearing into the mist.

Glory picked up the delicate gift and rested it in her palm.

"How *spectacular*," she whispered.

Chapter Five

To the sound of Mrs Quick totting up her cash on the other side of the curtain, Glory uncupped her left hand to reveal the crow's gift. Balancing it on the small hook that protruded from the tip of her wooden forefinger, she held it up to the lamp and watched it flicker ever so gently.

"A teardrop of liquid rainbow," she whispered and turned it clockwise to see its colours change. It was as strong as nails. What on earth could it be? "You're strong, so you are. Yet so dainty." Even more so now that it sat upon her too-large wooden hand. Despite hours of sanding and filing, this war-time cast-off was never designed to fit a twelve-year-old; she ate all her greens and downed her daily spoonful of cod liver oil in the hope that she would grow faster and become a better match for it.

Keeping her finger still, she gathered the unwanted brooch and beads that had fallen from Mrs Quick's hot-tempered grip and placed the crow's gift alongside, willing it to stay put with the palm of her hand. She pulled a piece of paper and pencil from a drawer and began to sketch.

Using light pencil strokes, she drew the crow's teardrop in the centre, complete with swirls of light and shade and surrounded it with row after row of beads until they met the loops of the gold filigree oval frame. Although it was only drawn on dull, white paper with a grey pencil, it looked so shiny and, quite definitely, *spectacular*.

With her tongue between her lips, she wasted no time and quickly reassembled her newly designed brooch.

Soon, she was done. It *was* spectacular, Glory assured herself, so much so it made her cheeks redden and her chin rise. She made that. She, Miss Gloria Bobbin, was its creator – there was now a thing of real beauty before her that would be part of this world all because of her. But she quickly came to her senses and frowned; it was spectacular to the eye but, as she expected, when she turned it over to secure its pin, three beads fell and rolled across the desk.

Glory's nostrils flared, her jaw stiffened and her unruly red curls fell from behind her ears. "Drats! Drats! Darn this clumsy hand," she growled, stomping her foot and banging her wooden fist on the desk.

"What's going on in there? Not seen and *not* heard is the rule, need I remind you, you stupid brat."

"Oh, shush with your stupid rules," Glory wanted to say but, instead, bit her lip. She scowled in rage. But her rage wasn't directed at the fallen beads or her hardnosed mistress. It wasn't even aimed at her wooden hand – it was entirely directed at herself for being such a short tempered fool, bringing Mrs Quick's unwanted threats by banging her fist on the table like that; nine times out of ten, it was her inability to *not* do or say what she was thinking that got her into trouble.

"Sorry, Mrs Quick. Eh… it's just a rat, back here. Do stay safe there while I have it leave!"

"A rat? NO!"

"A very, very large one, Mrs Quick!

"In my emporium? GET RID OF IT!" Mrs Quick

forgot about counting her fistful of coins and threw them across her mahogany counter.

Glory gathered the three runaway beads and quickly placed them back in the brooch, all the while sniggering as she heard Mrs Quick's coins roll, pause, and hit the polished floorboards; some spinning to a stop and others rolling further still.

"My money!" cried Mrs Quick and it was soon followed by a rapid slap and thud of palms and knees across the floor as she chased her loot. With one eye at the curtain's edge, Glory peeked out and bit down hard on her apron's shoulder strap as another snigger threatened to escape.

A runaway coin rolled under the curtain and spun to a halt at the toe of Glory's boot. "See a penny, pick it up – all day long, you'll have good luck," she whispered. As she squeezed it into her bag, the bells above the door jangled.

Mrs Quick jumped to her feet, turning to face the door mid-rise. The spindly heel of her shoe caught the hem of her tasselled dress. Glory heard the sounds of a lengthy rip and airborne eye-glasses pinging off a glass cabinet door.

"Madam?"

"Sir! Welcome! Do forgive me," said Mrs Quick as she hid the torn silk at her waist with one hand and pulled the loose lock of greying hair from her eyes with the other. "Just examining the floor. My useless girl missed a spot. HUSH Maximus!" she snapped, annoyed that her dog chose now to rise from his velvet cushion and unwelcome a guest with a growl.

"*Useless girl?* Old bat," Glory whispered and edged closer to the curtain's gap – a gap just wide enough to see their gentleman visitor raise an eyebrow, remove his top hat and slowly peel off his gloves. He placed them into the bowl of his hat and offered it all to Mrs Quick before turning his back. He studied the contents of the glass cabinets above Maximus, making sure to tip his toe against the dog's paw.

"You know who I am?"

"Indeed, sir. It's a pleasure to see you, Mr eh…" Mrs Quick was struggling. She squinted and grabbed at her empty eye-glasses chain wrapped around her neck. She edged closer to her guest.

"*Lord.*" Before Glory knew it, she had whispered it as loud as she could through the curtain. Of course, by no means did Mrs Quick deserve her help but, short of barging onto the shop floor to take control of Mrs Quick's cringe-worthy attempts to impress, she would do her bit to save the emporium's reputation and, quite frankly, her only chance of a job. "He's a Lord," she whispered again, just to be sure.

"Lord? Yes, eh, welcome, Lord...?" Mrs Quick backed up towards the curtain and questioned the wooden finger that threatened to pull it wide open, the shame of which Mrs Quick simply could not tolerate.

"*Buckram*," added Glory.

Mrs Quick twitched with her sharp intake of air. "Of course. Lord Buckram." She threw his hat and gloves on the counter less than pleasantly and sprang to secure the curtain either side with her hands. "What may we do for you today?" She offered a curtsey and hissed at Glory to stay back through the velvet.

"I would not normally waste my time frequenting such frivolous emporia," he said and flicked a beaded tassel that hung from a necklace display in the window. "However, it is necessary I see to this in person, it being of such importance. My clients have assured me that this is the *only* jewellery emporium, in Inthington and beyond, capable of producing the desired quality. You have a reputation for perfection, so it seems." He quickly scanned the contents of the cabinet before him. "Though I imagine I will need some convincing," he added under his breath.

"Ooh, dear Mr… Lord, you do flatter me so." Mrs Quick fluttered her matted lashes and patted the loops of beads that dangled down her chest.

Glory winced. Lord Buckram was not in the business of gifting flattery; he was the serious and successful owner of Inthington's glorious Millbank Gallery and had little time for anything other than being all important.

"Can you or can you not?" he replied in one tone. He turned to make eye contact with Mrs Quick.

"Can I, Lord?" she squeaked.

"Provide quality? Exceptional, outstanding, astonishing quality."

"Why, of course. May I interest you in some cufflinks, Lord Buckram?" Mrs Quick fiddled through her ring of keys, now tangled with the loose threads of her waistband.

Lord Buckram replied with a flick of his hand.

"Or a choker necklace, perhaps? For the delightful lady in your life?"

Glory kicked Mrs Quick's heel through the curtain. "No!" she said, quiet as a mouse and shook her head in amazement that Mrs Quick should surely know more about the public and private lives of Inthington's most elite.

"I do not seek such frippery. I require a handcrafted item that is nothing less than spectacular. It will be a gift I shall present, as I have in my possession an urgent letter announcing the arrival of a rather important gentleman. Of course, I shall be hosting a grand ball at my gallery to celebrate his latest invention. I trust, although I have my doubts," he lowered his tone, "that you have *some* knowledge of the name *Master Sharp*?"

Glory covered her mouth with her palm.

The mere mention of the great man's name caused Mrs Quick's ankle to give way. She steadied herself and stared back at Lord Buckram. "Did you say... OH!" Her head trembled.

"I require a handcrafted walking cane, for as you are aware, Master Sharp, the gentleman that he is, is rarely seen without."

"*Indeed*," replied Mrs Quick, the word sounding twice its given length, "and quite the trend it has become, too. Why, we have a fabulous selection of canes." Glory heard the click of Mrs Quick's heels as she limped over to the far corner, each step punctuated with the woman's wittering of Master Sharp's name. There was a shuffle and a drag of something heavy across the floor. Glory pinched open the curtain to see Mrs Quick present a mahogany display box stuffed with a selection of silver-headed and diamond-adorned sticks.

"Is this the best you can do?"

"These? Eh, no!" Mrs Quick nervously replied. "These were crafted by our apprentices. Riff-raff attempts, I agree." She dismissed the lot with a quick wave.

"The cheek!" Glory's squeak was out of her mouth before she could stop it.

Without moving his head, Lord Buckram eyeballed the curtain and the wooden finger that cornered it.

"Ahem, over here! HERE!" cried Mrs Quick as though she was encouraging an escaped hound back to her. She did, however, succeed in regaining the Lord's attention, and kicked Maximus away from her feet. "What you require is the work of our *Master* Craftsman, Inthington's finest artisan."

"May I inspect a sample of his work?"

"*Her* work," corrected Mrs Quick. She raised her bony arms out to the side and bowed as though she was centre stage at an opera. "I shall be honoured to create your walking cane with my own hands."

Glory hissed behind the curtain and shook her head. She was yet to see Mrs Quick create anything other than stinking cigarette smoke and constant grief.

"Indeed. May I inspect a sample of *your* work?" requested Lord Buckram less than patiently.

Mrs Quick's finger automatically pointed towards the various cabinets filled with headbands, necklaces, bangles and accessories of glittering quality.

Lord Buckram raised his eyebrows, blew a quick breath out through his nostrils and walked towards the counter to retrieve his hat and gloves.

"Ah, heck," whispered Glory. This was a shambles. One of Inthington's finest men was on the shop floor, pockets bursting with money and fame! Lord Buckram and Master Sharp might as well be the King and Queen around these parts. Creating a piece for this great man to give to, quite possibly, the world's *greatest* man, would put this emporium on the world map. It would put *her* name on the map – or maybe not at all – but her job would be safe, her sister's rent tin would be full and her dream of owning her own emporium… She shook her dreamy thoughts away and took a deep breath.

"Lord Buckram?" Glory's muffled voice came from behind the curtain.

"NO! That's nothing! Just my scrubber girl!" Mrs Quick ran past him and slapped the curtain. Glory, hidden on the other side, stumbled and did well to keep her new teardrop brooch in its red velvet display box safe in the palm of her hand.

"Mrs Quick!" Glory hissed.

Mrs Quick put her head around the curtain. "Shut it. If he sees that my Master Craftsman is nothing more than a one-handed, uneducated girl, I will be doomed."

Despite that, Glory handed Mrs Quick the box. It was received with a gulp.

"Why, here we go, Lord Buckram," Mrs Quick said as she floated over to his side, "a fine example of my craftsmanship." She held the box up to his face. "Let me remove it…"

Glory coughed, hoping Mrs Quick would interpret that as a no-it-will-fall-apart.

"Eh, rather, let us admire it in its glorious splendour

as it rests in its gift box, complete with plush velvet and..."

Lord Buckram grabbed his hat and gloves and marched to the door. "January 6th, deliver the cane to my office in the Millbank Gallery. Master Sharp shall arrive at eight o'clock sharp to launch his new invention. Do *not* be late."

Mrs Quick's mouth fell open.

The bells jangled as Lord Buckram swung open the emporium's front door. "Spectacular," he muttered to himself and he was gone.

Chapter Six

"Do you know who Master Sharp is?" asked Glory. "Hop once for yes, twice for no."

The crow pecked at the scattering of crumbs that fell either side of the heel of nutty bread as it landed on the pavestones. It cleared one side so it hopped, once, over the heel and devoured all on that side too.

"Ha! One hop! I knew you'd understand my words, Fusspot! So, tell me all you know!" Glory giggled and wiped crumbs from her lap. She grasped her wooden hand and pulled her knees close to her chest.

"Master Sharp, Fusspot. He's no normal gentleman," she said as she stared up into the misty morning sky. "He's a maker of things – things never before seen or heard of. If he sees a way to make things better, he goes and dreams up the best machine for the job.

They say it all started when he'd find an old nail or scrap of metal and he'd wonder: what did it come from? Was it still working without it? So he'd go and build it a new machine. Now he's the most famous inventor in all the world." Glory nodded at the crow. "And he's coming to Inthington."

The crow returned to the heel of nutty bread. Its strong beak lifted it easily and it stretched out both wings.

"In a rush? Me too. Mrs Quick has called a meeting for eight o'clock sharp." She sniggered and stood up from the damp step. "A meeting! Did you ever? That old bag only has me – I'm the only fool to stick around longer than a week. There's only so much ear-battering a person can take…" Glory sighed and wiped her wooden hand dry with the corner of her shawl, "unless you have one of these, of course." She was silent for a moment but, for fear of sounding pitiful, she kicked at the pavestones and scowled.

It was ironic that throughout her childhood she was reminded to stand up for herself. In fact, because she was born without a right hand, she would need to do more standing up than anyone else in all of Inthington. But, as soon as she had secured her apprenticeship at *the* emporium, standing up was forbidden. She was reminded, time and again, how she was so blessed to have such an opportunity. But *not* standing up for herself felt fake and wooden, just like her fake and wooden hand.

The crow pulled in its wings and stood still.

"Enough of that, Fusspot," said Glory, dismissing her own thoughts. "I shall see you this afternoon – and I'll have a nice surprise for you!"

Glory watched the crow take flight, bread in beak. Turning the old key, she pushed up the rusted latch of Frippery & Fandangle's back door; a far cry from the shiny brass knob that adorned the front entrance on Crossgrain Street.

"Golden rule number one thousand: never use the front door, always the back," Glory huffed as she rubbed rust from the palm of her hand. But there was one thing that made up for the dull back entrance: just inside, the wall to the right of the corridor was covered from floor to ceiling with countless mahogany drawers. Each drawer had a small, square façade but, when removed entirely, it was the length of an arm. A brass frame, labelled with the script of Mrs Quick's ancestors, and a cut-glass knob twinkled on each one, even in the limited light from the door's round window.

Glory made it her business to read another label each morning and pull the drawer to see what treasures lay within. Trinkets and titbits, pearls and gemstones; several of her favourite things were already found inside and who knows how long they had been there, waiting to be used – the emporium had been trading for more years than she could imagine.

"*Charms*," she said as she ran her finger along a label, "what do you hide in there?" She pulled the glass knob firmly; the drawer hung on tight for a moment before sliding open. The narrow drawer balanced on her wrist and up along her arm. Twirling the contents around with the tips of her wooden fingers, her forefinger's hook caught its first charm: a delightful pewter shoe, no bigger than a fingernail. Rather than pocket it, she discarded it back into the drawer. "Sorry, you're *unlucky*," she told it. "Shoes on a table are a sign of death. Even if you were hanging from my wrist and I leaned on my desk, you'd bring bad luck." She searched for another.

"CHILD!"

"Coming, Mrs Quick!" She noisily replaced the

drawer, hid her pouch bag beneath her shawl and made her way into her workshop, annoyed that her heart felt it necessary to pound.

The smoke of several cigarettes filled the room and a stiff Mrs Quick sat perched on the edge of Glory's desk. She repeatedly flicked the mouthpiece of her ebony cigarette holder with her thumbnail.

"Am I late, Mrs Quick?" asked Glory, nervously. She blinked her stinging eyes several times.

"Stupid girl. I do not have time for pointless chatter."

"Sorry, Mrs Quick," replied Glory, knowing Mrs Quick meant to answer *no* but, for whatever reason, felt that would be too kind.

Mrs Quick sucked in a lungful of smoke and blew it out slowly, staring at Glory. When she was done, she spoke with a gravelly voice. "Including today, you have four days to produce this walking cane. And should that Master Sharp choose to fancy himself up with it, it will guarantee the success of this establishment for ever." She stood up and towered over her apprentice. "*THE Master Sharp*," she spat. "Let me be clear, Gloria…" She said no more, but bared her long teeth. On her return to the shop floor,

Mrs Quick whipped the velvet curtain shut and spent longer than necessary poking at its sides so not even an ant could peek through.

Glory silently mouthed every sinful, wicked word she could think of. She looked at her desk and whispered, "Start somewhere." She needed some encouragement, like anyone would when faced with the impossible. She had four days to design and assemble Master Sharp's walking cane. Although time was tight, it wasn't so much the issue – she was well used to tight deadlines, rushing being her speciality. It was the brief that bothered her. Yes, she could make something that looked the part, but something that would withstand the weight of such a powerful man? She could recall Lord Buckram's words easily and they were causing a thumping headache; he demanded *spectacular*, not to mention *exceptional*, *outstanding* and *astonishing quality*.

She wasn't surprised by his demands – her father once said Lord Buckram was a *perfectionist*, and that meant he expected the absolute best from everyone and everything. "Lord Buckram says if you want success, go and make it but make it right."

Glory cleared her desk, pulled out several pieces

of paper and used her father's small pocket-knife to sharpen her pencil. As the nib sharpened, the knife's handle began to hold heat from her hand and, when she was done, she pressed the metal against her lips. "Warm, but not hot," she said. Never again would it hold such searing heat as when it was held in her father's skilled hand as he carved her a rose, a figurine or an apple from wood – so flawlessly she'd swear she could smell their perfume or touch their skin. *Perfection.* Faced with a blank page, she began to sketch her thoughts and wishes for the handle of the great walking cane.

Soon, the doorbell jangled and, before it settled, it rang again, and again. Glory crept up to the curtain and used her wooden finger to pull it back just enough to see three customers, two with daughters in tow, fanning their chilled faces with gilt edged cards – invitations to the Sharp Ball where Master Sharp would reveal his latest invention. Mrs Quick stood centre of attention, clicking her long nails with her thumbnail.

"*Naturally*, ladies," chimed Mrs Quick, "Lord Buckram was thrilled when I suggested we craft a gift for my good friend, *Master Sharp*," she lied.

"It wouldn't seem right for such a man to be seen without at least one of our pieces, don't you agree, Mrs Selvage? He has a reputation to uphold after all." She removed the lady's coat from her shoulders and fingered one of last season's Frippery & Fandangle brooches that flattened its fur. "Now what can we do for you today? We mustn't dilly dally; my craftsmen await me – diamond selection, ruby measuring and whatnot," said Mrs Quick with a wave of her hand towards the curtain.

Glory laughed, louder than she had probably intended, and soon wished she could take it back – Mrs Selvage's daughter was staring her way. Glory let go of the curtain. As it rippled, she gulped; she was the same sour-faced girl who was one year ahead of her in school. A right trouble-maker. She was thirteen at most, and was more than capable of exposing a one-handed, younger-than-sixteen, school-expelled girl.

"What's this, Mummy dear?" The girl's sickly sweet voice was hardly audible over the sound of her fancy shoes as she approached the curtain. Curious, Glory peeked out through the gap and watched her stall within arm's reach.

"Mummy's busy, Rosie darling. Now, to answer your question, Mrs Quick…"

Rosie grinned and ran her finger along a row of fine gold chains that hung neatly from a brass display unit on the counter. As they tangled, she pushed one free of its hanger and dangled it on her white-gloved finger. "Oops," she said, aimed directly at Glory's near-hidden face. Cocksure, Rosie Selvage slipped the gold chain into her own pocket.

"Oi!" cried Glory. She whipped the curtain wide open. "Mrs Quick! She's after nicking your—"

"Look at what we have here, Mummy!" said the girl, voice loud and overlapping Glory's accusation with ease. "There's a *child* making jewellery in there, eleven or twelve I'd say – with one hand! How funny!"

Mrs Selvage dropped her invitation to the ground. "A *child*?"

Mrs Quick roared with laughter, no doubt buying herself time to consider an excuse. She reached the curtain in two steps. "Thank you, Gloria, for bringing lunch for your uncle, my *Master Craftsman*."

"But she's robbing stuff, Mrs—"

"Off home with you now," Mrs Quick said less than

kindly and pushed Glory backwards. She whipped the curtain closed, hiding herself and her apprentice from their visitors. Pulling Glory's stool closer to the curtain, she grabbed a pencil and paper and forced Glory to sit. "*Eleven?*" she barked.

"I am *not* eleven, I'm twel… I mean, sixteen—"

"Sit and take notes and don't open your filthy mouth unless spoken to. In keeping with your reduced age, you get *half*. Do you hear me? Your wages are cut in half," she spat through gritted teeth. "You are *this* close," she said, holding her fingers between them.

With a racing heart, a rent tin to fill and a career in her plans, all Glory could do was sit. *Half*. She would have to work twice the hours to make up for it. When the curtain closed, she stuck out her tongue. "Stupid girl," she spluttered, not sure if it was aimed at herself or the thieving girl with her perfect blonde hair and royal-blue, gold-buttoned coat.

After a convincing apology from Mrs Quick, the shoppers discussed their desires for the upcoming ball and conversations of colour schemes and shoes, pearls and diamonds, feathered headbands and lipstick holders soon filled the shop floor. The tantalising items in the display cabinets were admired but quickly dismissed; they were ideal for Inthington's wild flapper dances and parties. The Sharp Ball, however, demanded more – only individually made, perfectly co-ordinated embellishments would do.

"Aquamarine and gold," snapped one lady, "by Gabrielle Chanel, of course. A floor-length dress although it's rather boyish in style... it's all the fashion. My feather boa is a mix of the same colours with a few peacock, so I desire a complementary headband; something original and never before seen."

Glory drew two lines across her paper and began filling the spaces with each customer's specific requests. Just as one customer departed, another arrived, and so it continued until Glory heard the clock strike twelve. She shook her aching fingers and was relieved when Mrs Quick bid farewell to the last customer and held the door shut, like plugging a leak.

"Maximus needs to stretch his legs, Gloria, I shall be but one minute," she said as she struggled with her overcoat and fur hat. Glory heard the click of the key in the lock after the front door slammed.

"Fusspot!" cried Glory. She fished her pouch bag

out from beneath her apron and ran to the back door. The crow was waiting for her, balancing on the back of the garden chair. White flecks dotted its feathers.

"Snow!" Glory circled the table and chairs with her arms out wide. She turned her face to the sky, opened her mouth and stuck out her tongue. Soon, a fluffy flake landed on the tip of her tongue and she giggled out loud.

The crow squawked in return and shook its wings free of their dusting.

"You poor divil, Fusspot! You must be freezing. Never fear, I have something that will warm the cockles of your heart." Glory, now also feeling the cold, untied the tassel of her bag with her purple-tipped fingers. She placed a slice of cake on the table and scooped crumbs out from beneath her ragdoll at the bottom of her bag.

"Here, nibble on these," she said and held out her cupped hand, now dotted with yellow crumbs. "That there is Lemon Pound cake. My sister made it for the tearoom in Fitzroy's – one of Inthington's best hotels."

The crow leaned over and tried a crumb. It soon

came forward for more. Glory smiled but her hand trembled and she sighed. The crow stopped pecking and looked sideways.

"I'm in a muddle, Fusspot. The old hag has gone and cut my wages in half. That's half the money but twice the work with this great ball. You should have seen the number of customers that arrived this morning, all wanting the impossible," she said and gave the bird a detailed account of the orders. "And I have to make a walking cane that knocks the socks off Master Sharp. How the heck will I do it? With *this* useless thing?" She waved her wooden hand in the air. "Everything just falls apart, and if I lose this job…"

The crow preened a feather in its chest, marched over to the slice of cake, took it and flew away.

"Bye," said Glory but it was well gone by then.

It was after dark when Mrs Quick pulled back the curtain. Glory looked up from her papers and watched her hobble over to the side of the desk where she leaned and stayed until the rows and rows of tassels on her dress stopped swaying. Her stiff shoulders had slackened, Glory noticed, and a red glow beamed from her hard cheeks. In her hand was a large bag of cash, tied with twine. She dropped it to the floor with a thud.

"How many?"

Glory quickly totted up the orders. "I count ten, Mrs Quick!"

"Yes, ten," she replied almost dreamily.

"Ten! Oh, Mrs Quick, you must agree this is not possible and I will need—"

Mrs Quick threw her head back and laughed. It went on and on, even when she had straightened her head and stared back at Glory. She wrinkled her nose when she was done.

Glory squeezed her fingers into a fist and felt ready to punish herself for thinking Mrs Quick would ever be reasonable.

"If you fail me on this… if as much as one bead falls from its clasp, *one*, you will never work in this town again. And you are gravely mistaken if you think it stops there; think about your dear sister…" Mrs Quick picked up her sack of coins and removed her coat and hat from their hook.

"Dee-Dee?"

"She works for the Fitzroy Hotel, I believe? One of my favourites. Although, I do wonder if I should have reason to complain to the owner about that awful baker girl in his employment…"

Glory watched her march over to Maximus, tuck him into her coat and smother him with ridiculous sharp pecks. It took fifteen steps, Glory counted, for Mrs Quick to depart and slam the door shut for the night. And for each step she felt her heart thump.

"You're a rotten soul!" cried Glory, "You're a horrible, mean, selfish woman. If you ever go near my sister, I'll go straight to your Master Sharps and your

Lord Buckrams and tell them exactly what you are – you're a *fake*."

When she was done shouting to the empty shop, she stood and waited for her breathing to settle before she grabbed her hat and shawl and turned out the lights. Using the small chink of moonlight that bounced off each glass drawer knob, she walked along the dark corridor that led to the back door.

She rose on her tiptoes and looked out the round window. Heavy snow was still falling and it gave the dark yard a wonderful cyan carpet. Wrapping her shawl tight, she stepped out into the night. She listened to the crunch of snow underfoot and, for a moment, circled where she stood, flattening the glistening snow with her boots.

That's when she heard it: a tinkle by her foot. She bent over and saw moonlight bounce off something shiny. Using her wooden hand for comfort, she scooped up a handful of snow and there, half buried in the centre, was a most glorious thing: a circle of gold filigree, almost as thin as thread and twisted like petals, with clear glass stones set in a circle around fine white china. Glory wiped the icy cold surface with her thumb and there, on the white, appeared the outline of a bird in ultramarine blue. Glory tilted it towards the moonlight – it was a gloriously hand-painted peacock.

She had never seen the likes of it before.

Glory looked to the ground and spotted the tiny pattern of thin marks in the snow around the gap where her treasure once lay. In a split second, she knew what to do.

"Thank you, Fusspot. One order down, nine to go."

Chapter Seven

"CAREFUL!" snapped Mrs Quick. "More to the left. *Left*. There. Now do *not* touch it."

Glory stood back from the new display cabinet that, after hard work on her part, now sat in the middle of the emporium's floor. It was well after closing time and, with only two days to go before the Sharp Ball, Mrs Quick had arranged delivery of a most wonderful cabinet to house the fruits of Glory's hardest working day: ten glorious embellishments, perfectly assembled in their red velvet boxes, with plenty of room for one yet-to-be-crafted walking cane.

The shop was richly lit with brass lamps and their light reflected off the rectangular cabinet's dome of glass as it curved down the sides and met with its wide base of rich mahogany. Along the front, etched in beautiful script and adorned with swags and ribbons, Glory read the words *Frippery & Fandangle Emporium*, and beneath, in matter-of-fact lettering, *Master Craftsmen of Bespoke Embellishments*. The cabinet was hip-height and any items lucky enough to be displayed within could be viewed from any angle.

Glory wiped the sweat off her face and stood next to Mrs Quick. As Maximus sniffed each clawed foot of the cabinet, Glory recalled this one time at home when she'd sketched a powerful lady and spent hours perfecting her curls and jewellery and even the wrinkles around her determined eyes. Her father was so proud, he carved her a magnificent picture frame overnight. He asked everyone to sit around the table and he silently opened the frame's casing and placed her drawing inside, face down.

Glory remembered the moment her motivation to create was born: it was that very second he turned the frame around and there was so much pride in that room, she could feel it in her cheeks.

And now, before her, in the shape of a cabinet, was another frame. Mrs Quick, despite all her horribleness, knew a thing or two about making things look spectacular and, now that she was happy with the position of her new furniture, she slapped her hands and instructed Glory to fill it to the brim with the orders for the Sharp Ball.

Glory collected the first piece from the workshop and placed the small red velvet box into the cabinet. Having flipped open the lid of the box, she took the soft paintbrush she held between her teeth and gently brushed away any imaginary dust from the exquisite brooch.

Mrs Quick came closer and stood peering over Glory's shoulder. She was purring and Glory took that as a compliment.

"Bring me more." She snatched the paintbrush from Glory's hand. "Bring them all."

Glory returned to the workshop and selected the box with the peacock headband – the main ingredient of which being one of Fusspot's earliest gifts. When she pulled back the curtain, she found Mrs Quick head deep in the cabinet with hips and bony elbows jiggling.

"Those gems ain't going nowhere," said Glory. Mrs Quick jerked up, flicking the fuzzed-up brush to the floor. Despite Mrs Quick's doubt and her ferocious brushing, every part of that piece was secure – Glory was sure of that. It and every other piece had, after all, survived its journey in Fusspot's beak over the course of one long night. All it took was her imagination and some tweaking to produce the finished products – no rolling beads, no fist banging, no leg stomping, and no blaming her clumsy hand.

"May I?" asked Glory as she dared to demand more space to place her next piece in the cabinet.

Mrs Quick stumbled on the discarded brush and stood to one side. Glory angled the peacock headband next to the brooch and smirked. Ha! The old bat was impressed by her work! And surely that meant Mrs Quick *needed* her now.

With the last piece in place, Mrs Quick hovered over the treasure chest of sparkling silvers and golds that shone with polished sea-glass, hand-painted ceramics and antique gems. Glory studied Mrs Quick's rare smile.

"To your satisfaction, Mrs Quick?" she asked, enjoying the pleasing feeling of confidence that came with her pride.

Mrs Quick responded by lighting her cigarette and taking the longest of drags to compose herself. "Where is the walking cane? Where? WHERE?"

Glory tutted. TEN! Ten orders completed in one very long day and not as much as a thank you from the old bat. "Yes, yes, hold onto your knickers – your cane is coming." She urged Mrs Quick to calm down with her hand.

Mrs Quick's eyes bulged.

"Get back to work. And do *not* think that, because you and your man-hand have delivered on these... these *simple* pieces, you can speak to me like that, you—"

"And if you want your cane made, maybe you shouldn't speak to *me* like that!"

Mrs Quick swiftly turned her back to Glory and placed both palms flat on the counter's polished surface. Glory frowned as Mrs Quick's head drooped so low it disappeared behind her hunched shoulders and her dress's rows of tassels, that hung in perfect lines from her head to the floor, began to tremble.

Glory kicked the back of her own heel. Here we go! Thanks to her unstoppable big mouth, Mrs Quick was going to fly into an ear-battering rage. Glory quickly scampered back into the workshop, closing the curtain behind her. She wished more than ever that it was made of stone to seal Mrs Quick out.

Several minutes later, she heard Maximus yelp as he was yanked from his bed and dragged out to the street. As soon as the emporium's door slammed, Glory breathed out a long breath – perhaps, for once, she really did have the upper hand, however long that might last.

Before she left for the night, Glory cleared her desk and placed across it a brand new, unadorned oak stick. There was no avoiding it now – the time had come to finally tackle it. She pinned her sketches along the edge of the shelf to her left and studied each for a moment. They were full of detail, down to a hair's breadth, with only the very tip of the cane yet to be considered and sketched.

Like the tassels on Mrs Quick's dress, something inside Glory trembled – and she wasn't sure if it was a feeling of excitement or a feeling of nerves. Somehow, Fusspot had delivered something wonderful for each of the ten orders. Indeed, it took her own skills to adapt them into the perfect embellishments that matched their brief but, much to her relief, the bulk of the frustrating and fiddly assembly was done. However, the pieces delivered in Fusspot's beak were dainty and light. The walking cane would be a different beast altogether; it needed to shout power and be a solid piece of art. And that was not something that could be plucked by a bird, from wherever it most definitely had accidentally fallen.

Glory wrapped herself up warm, tied the red ribbon of her hat loosely under her chin and opened the back door. Several inches of fresh snow covered the ground and she sighed when she saw no trace of Fusspot's footprints and no shiny new gifts. She would have to go it alone tomorrow and that thought frightened her.

Having tapped the latch down with her wooden hand and turned the rusted key with the other, she spun around only to fall back against the door as Fusspot flapped wildly at her skirt.

"There you are!" cried Glory.

She jumped in her skin – there was an echo, of sorts. Glory was sure of it; another voice had spoken the very same words.

She held her next breath and, for a few seconds, all was quiet. It was a buffered silence, the one you only hear when everything is padded in powdery snow and not an echo should be heard.

"Who's there?"

Her question was not aimed at the bird but it answered in its own way by rising from the ground and flapping its wings. It grabbed the red ribbon of Glory's hat and tugged and swooped before her, dragging her closer to the garden gate.

"FUSSPOT!" cried Glory.

"MAGPIE!" cried another.

In Elsetime

– 4th January 1928 –

Twelve-year-old Needle and young Glory Bobbin; living their lives in Inthington Town just a stone's throw from each other but with many decades between.

And so they meet.

Chapter Eight

Needle ducked left and right, trying to see through the emporium's gate where flapping wings and red ribbon made their way along the garden path towards him. He shot his arms through the gate's bars, stretching as far as he could go, and slapped some feathery part of Magpie.

"Drop it, you rascal," he ordered.

Magpie only let go of the hat's ribbon when Needle and Glory were face-to-face and close enough for their misty breaths to clash in the chilly air.

Just for a moment, all sound disappeared. The thick layer of snow made everything around them, from the pavestones to the gnarly branches that climbed the walls, a shade of the quietest blue. Frost glistened on the vertical bars of the gate between them and, slowly, Needle pulled back his dangling arms and grasped the cold bars.

"Don't you dare come in here or I will belt you!" warned Glory.

Needle gasped when he saw her wooden hand, now stretched out before her like a weapon. Should he run? He really didn't know – being faced with a person was hard enough, but being faced with one not so pleased was a big worry. Might she attack? Should he say something? Much like with those bakery thugs who'd pulled at his lips, keeping his mouth shut might add fuel to her fire. Not sure what to do, he slowly slipped his shivering hand back through the bars, gently grabbed the tips of her wooden fingers and shook them – just like his mother had taught him to do when faced with a stranger. And this girl, in Needle's opinion, was surely strange.

"Needle Luckett. How'd you do?" His voice was odd; a quiet bag of nerves and shivers. He'd practised introducing himself at home but never imagined he'd be face-to-face with a stranger without his father standing in between. He pulled back his hand, wiped his dripping nose and hugged his warm satchel.

Shivering, he watched Glory as she looked him up

and down. He was exactly her height but he knew she'd think he looked thin and his legs spindly thanks to his father's boots – one laced up in a tangled mess and the other flapped open. He was sure his face was reasonably clean but, with one sock on and the other off, his ripped shirt and patched-up trousers would scream one thing to her – and he could read that in her softening face; she was thinking this poor rag of a boy needed help. Perhaps he did.

"Well, Needle Luckett, you're probably hungry. Yes?" Glory rummaged in her bag and pulled out a finger of shortbread. She held it on her wooden palm and offered it to him. "I'm Gloria Bobbin – Glory."

Needle stared at Glory's freckled face and smiled. Her red curls stuck out at odd angles from under her hat and, although she had said very little, she was possibly the most colourful thing he had heard. He wasn't in the slightest bit hungry – fear had lined his stomach with daggers – but he had a million questions he needed to ask.

"No, not hungry, but… can you… can I… I don't be knowing…" he said as he rubbed the space between his eyebrows. "Sorry, miss, I banged my head something awful."

Glory squinted at the dirty bruise and raised bump on his forehead. "That, I can see. You need something for it," she said and threw the shortbread to the ground. "Fusspot, it's your lucky day."

"That be Magpie – and she ain't no fusspot. A pie of toenails would do her!"

"Actually," said Glory, throwing her eyes up to the heavens, "you are wrong. This here is a crow, *my* crow. Magpies have black and white feathers – you know: one for sorrow, two for joy? Do a twirl, Fusspot – see, all black." She lifted the latch on the gate and swung her wooden hand to welcome him in.

He didn't budge.

"You *can* come in."

Needle held up his finger and, if he'd had the courage, he'd have declared war – Magpie was his and there was no doubt about that.

"Ah-AH!" Glory stopped him before he began. "IN!"

Needle, annoyed with himself for never finding the right words out of the jumble of thoughts in his head, cranked his neck forward, crinkled up his nose and squinted his eyes. He studied her face; the freckled girl with the most colourful voice had just spoken like a bossy grown-up – maybe he was mistaken in thinking she was his age. Perhaps the sight of a wrinkle would put him straight.

"Are you coming in or what?" She cheekily imitated his scrunched up face and finished by sticking out her tongue. No, she wasn't a grown-up – that much was clear. "I *can* help you, you know," she added, gently.

Needle felt his eyes fill with tears – he wasn't sure why but reckoned it had something to do with being offered a helping hand, be it wooden or not. He felt utterly lost – a strange feeling considering he'd somehow recognised every road and laneway he'd taken to get here. He'd followed Magpie's trail until they'd arrived at this gate where he now stood freezing, worried and beyond confused. Deciding that the offer of help was difficult to refuse, he obeyed her orders and followed her to the back door of the emporium, keeping a polite distance between them.

When the key clicked in the lock, Glory turned to Needle and eyeballed him up close. "WAIT THERE." She pointed her wooden finger to the ground.

Needle nudged his feet forward to ensure he stood in the exact spot as instructed and watched her tiptoe along the dark corridor. Without any light, she disappeared somewhere at the end, but soon reappeared when the corridor was lit up so suddenly it made him jump.

"You're in luck – Mrs Cranky-pants is gone for the night," said Glory as she marched back to where he stood. She paused before him and stared so hard into his eyes that he was forced to look everywhere but into hers. "Tell me you won't burgle the place."

"Nnnn… no, miss!"

"It's *Glory*, and please speak up. Are you telling tales? And how do I believe you?" She sounded so headmistress-like that he wouldn't have been surprised had she pulled a yardstick from her bag.

"Cross my heart." He spoke louder this time, pretty much like his father. With his quivering finger, he slowly drew a cross on his chest – along his heartless, right side.

Having noticed Needle mix up his lefts and rights, Glory wasn't surprised at all and a pitiful smile appeared on her lips. "Yes, that will do nicely." She walked along the corridor, sure-footed. Needle didn't follow and waited outside.

"Oh, for goodness' sake…" Glory returned to the

door and snagged the strap of his satchel with the hook on her wooden finger. "Move! This way."

Needle didn't object to being pulled along like a stubborn puppy – he was too engrossed by the floor-to-ceiling drawers and their sparkling glass knobs that lined the corridor. Above each knob, swirling letters grandly introduced the contents like they were at a royal party. At the end of the corridor, rather than turn left into what appeared to be a workshop, Glory dragged him into a storeroom, not much larger than his trove. It was a musty space, filled with empty display boxes, jars filled with the tiniest of tools and a large ceramic sink.

"Sit down, please. There," said Glory, after she'd unhooked him from her wooden finger and pointed to a three-legged stool. She reached over his head and pulled a string that dangled from a dusty standing lamp. Light beamed down on his head.

"WHOA!" Needle jumped up, banging his head off the glass lampshade. Like a huge drooping flower head, its petals of amber glass rocked from side to side. "How'd you do that?" he asked as he stared at the instant, flicker-less light, "and where be the flame?" Squinting as he peered up into its centre, he steadied the swinging shade with his muddy hands. He was captivated. One pane of glass fell and smashed by his feet. "Ah, sorry 'bout that, Miss Glory."

"Crikey, you've ants in your pants. You'd swear you've never seen electricity before." Tutting, she scooped up the glass with her wooden hand and placed it in the sink.

"Lectrisy, miss?" It must have been another word for magic.

"*Elec-tricity*. Now *sit*. You'll need something cold for that bump. Let me see…" Glory wasn't going to admit it, but she'd played at nurses and doctors for many years with her handmade ragdolls, so tending to Needle's injury should be no bother to her. She rummaged through the cupboard under the sink and found an old floor-cloth.

"It be all new to me, this el… elect… back home, light comes from candles and not from—" Needle grabbed his cheeks. It was all wrong! Everything was odd and so different to home! A spiky cold feeling spread from the tip of his head down to the pit of his stomach. Never before had he felt so lost, so desperately in need of help. "Oh, miss, do you know how I be getting home?" he pleaded as he watched

Glory turn an unusual looking indoor tap and soak the cloth in water.

"Where *is* home, Needle? Where do you live?" Glory spoke more slowly now, wondering if this poor boy before her was educated at all.

Needle wasn't sure how to answer. Yes, of course he knew his address – his mother made him say it over and over in case he should wander too far. He thought of his mother now – she'd be smiling with her eyes, telling him to *think* and that if he knows the answer, just say it. "I be from here – Inthington? Inthington Town?"

Glory nodded as she held the cloth to his head. "Whereabouts? Don't think I've seen you before. Think I'd remember," she added, quietly.

"I live here – with Mam and Da in one of them white cottages on Broidery Quay, down by Eyelet Bridge…"

"What cottages? Ain't no cottages there – only the gallery and shops… I think you think this place is elsewhere… you must be lost."

"No… well, yeah… but they *are* there, them cottages. This place ain't else*where*, it be… it be else…"

Glory waited for him to finish for many seconds

longer than she normally would but finally put her hands on her hips. "Well? Spit it out."

"Else… else*time*. This place is elsetime. My home *is* there in 1864 – that be the right year because Mam wrote it down for me."

"*Elsetime?* No such word," Glory jeered but wished she could take it back. He was a sorry state, trembling with his sad face and fiddling fingers. "Needle, I think you've done more damage to your head than you think. You do know it's 1928? And Eyelet Bridge is in the very centre of Inthington? Ain't no room for cottages there…"

"*1928?*" Needle managed. He rose to his feet, dropping the cold cloth to the floor. He paced the room like a trapped rat.

"Yes, it's 1928. I think you have your mama's numbers in a muddle – you were nowhere near born back in, what did you say? 1864? Sure you're much younger than me – I'm sixteen." She paused in search of a reaction. "What are you now? Ten?"

"Twelve," Needle corrected with an obvious frown and considered the green tone of her words – *sixteen my hat*.

"Oh, sorry," said Glory before clearing her

throat. "Me too," she admitted in little more than a whisper.

Needle wasn't sure if she was sorry for thinking he was so young or sorry she was pretending to be so much older than her age but, either way, he accepted her apology with a nod. He reached into his shirt pocket and pulled out the scrap of paper upon which his mother had written the year, 1864. "I be telling you... it is, I mean *was* 1864," he said as he handed her the paper with his quivering fingers, "Mam only wrote this yesterday."

"Right. That's enough. I think you need something colder for that head of yours." Glory carefully slid the paper back into Needle's pocket and turned to examine the contents of the cupboard in search of something soft but cool.

Needle stuck his grubby thumb and forefinger into his mouth and whistled so loud that Glory fell to her knees and rubbed her ears.

"Are you completely—" She stopped when she heard a sound from the corridor. "Mrs Quick!"

Her voice was the sharpest shade of orange: *fear*. Needle flapped his hand out before him. "No, no! Please don't be afraid, miss! It be only Magpie!" He bucked his teeth and pointed at his wiggling ears in an attempt to make her orange words blend into yellow; a clever trick that often made his mother giggle. Glory's frown told him to stop and he was glad when Magpie finally flapped her way into the room and stood to attention on his knee. He picked up the cloth and hung it gently on her beak.

"Bring me some snow, Magpie. Fill this up with it."

Glory sat silently, sucking a curl of her hair, and stared at Needle while Magpie returned to the snowy yard. But after less than a minute, she couldn't stay quiet any longer.

"You *do* know she's a crow?"

Needle nodded.

"So why would you do something so daft as call her a magpie?" Glory wasn't sure if the bump on his head wasn't to blame.

Needle shrugged but the look on Glory's face made it clear that wouldn't do. "When was the last time you heard someone call their dog *Dog*? *Rover*'s a better name, if he likes to go wandering. Or *Happy*, if he, you know, makes you happy. *Cat*'d even be a better name for a dog if he was a good mouser," he suggested with a smile. "See, I don't think it be right naming anyone by how they look." Glory swung her wooden hand behind her back. He paused. What names had *she* been called? "It… it's what they *do* that matters. That's why a fly is called a *fly* because what else do they be doing? They be experts at it."

Glory's shoulders suddenly relaxed. She remembered her father saying something very similar about why they chose to name her something so glorious as Gloria.

"Everyone knows them magpies be experts at stealing shiny things but our Magpie's the best treasure hunter of all – she'd spot a muddy penny's sparkle from a good mile, better than any magpie I know," he said and wondered if he was making any sense at all. When she smiled, he added, "She be a divil for robbing stuff too."

Magpie returned with a pouch of snow in her beak and settled on Needle's lap.

"Fine work," said Needle.

"She *is* yours, isn't she?"

"Yeah." Needle patted Magpie's tail feathers.

"So you were telling the truth about that?"

"Yeah."

Glory crawled over to Magpie and rubbed her cold

beak. "And the rest? About your home. Was that no lie?"

"I never told a lie in my life. Not one, Miss Glory." Needle straightened himself up, held the bag of snow against his forehead and stared deep into her eyes.

Once again, Glory accepted the stare; she didn't dismiss it, fiddle or make idle chat. That moment felt safe. And now, out of the frosty blue, they seemed to have made a special connection.

Chapter Nine

Glory's father's pocket-watch ticked near her ear all night long. She didn't dare wake up late – she had to get back to the emporium before Mrs Quick arrived. With the bed sheets pulled up high under her chin, she forced herself to wait until six o'clock before slipping out of bed, fully dressed.

She tiptoed her way down the stairs but there was no need to avoid its creaky third step; in fact, she could have danced on it, for her sister – already a couple of hours into her day's baking – did not work quietly. As Dee-Dee kneaded and slapped dough on the kitchen table, she sang, hummed and whistled as she worked. Drumming out the beat of the latest dance tunes worked wonders for her baking and Glory often wondered if this was the secret ingredient that made her sister's pastries and cakes the best in Inthington. The owners of the Fitzroy Hotel were blessed to have her as their baker.

Glory turned the knob of the kitchen door and, with squinted eyes, peeked in. From the darkness of the hallway, her father's hand-carved furniture and shelves stacked with his wooden jugs and bowls, all added warmth to the light. The air was filled with puffs of flour and line upon line of teacakes and sliced jam rolls were packed into a large box – all ready for her sister to deliver to the Fitzroy Hotel. It was a miniature factory squeezed into one small kitchen and in its centre, was its busy engine – Dee-Dee.

Her back was turned as she twisted strips of dough with each hand, two at a time. Today, she wore her father's old pinstriped pyjama bottoms, now transformed into what must have been the latest trend, and tied tight at the waist with a wide purple sash. A matching turban protected her short hair and, despite the tea-towel thrown across one shoulder, she looked dazzling and sure; as though she meant business. Glory knew, of course, that it wasn't her high fashion that made her appear so confident – she oozed it from every pore.

Glory tiptoed in, grabbed her usual and made for the door, but she hesitated – she had another mouth to feed this morning. "*Needle*," she mouthed. What would he make of her sister should they ever meet? Of course, by now he may have found his way home, wherever that was. But, just in case, she reached in for a sticky jam roll.

The whistling and dough-twisting stopped. "GLORIA BOBBIN, TAKE YOUR MUCKY PAWS OFF THOSE CAKES!" roared Dee-Dee. "You already have the one – what on earth are you up to, looking for another? You'll leave me short!"

"Sorry, Dee-Dee, I'm hungry. I didn't get any supper last night, I was working late."

Her sister's eyebrows relaxed and she wiped her hands on her tea-towel. "That Mrs Quick needs a talking to. She's working you too hard. Home near midnight and up before dawn… when you go in today, stand up to that woman and tell her you won't do it anymore. And tell her I am very cross!" She flicked her head but gave a knowing wink and a sympathetic smile – there was no way on this earth her younger sister should jeopardise her job by actually saying such things. "My poor little pet."

Glory smiled; despite Dee-Dee being only sixteen, Glory adored her sister's attempts at mothering. "It's only so busy because of the Sharp Ball – things will get easier after that... won't they, Dee-Dee?"

"True. The hotel has us working our fingers to the bone too – we're supplying all the food for this ball and they've left it to me to do the baking!" She spun around and shook her head at the mess of their kitchen. "I'll be busy at it from now until the ball. Even still, that Mrs Quick is asking too much of you – too much for any twelve-year-old. You know that, don't you?" She pushed Glory's hair behind her ears, not noticing how Glory's eyes stared everywhere but at hers – perhaps it was time to declare she would pay the price of half a wage for fibbing to Mrs Quick about her age.

"Apprenticeship, my eye," Dee-Dee continued, "I don't see *her* teaching *you* how to make jewellery. She's put it all on your shoulders. It's as bad as asking me to bake everything for the ball. *Singlehandedly!*" Dee-Dee lovingly rubbed Glory's wooden hand before twirling her little sister around beneath her raised arm. "Let's dance!" She kicked up her feet behind her to some Charleston beat only she could imagine and swung Glory's hands wildly to each side. "It's women like us who *really* run the world, you know that too, don't you?"

Glory nodded, freed a hand and reached for the Votes-for-Women badge pinned proudly to her sister's blouse. Glory thumb-wiped a layer of flour off its surface and Dee-Dee's dancing settled down to a gentle sway.

"After tomorrow night, can we do something nice together?" asked Glory. She took a sharp intake of breath on hearing her own words: *tomorrow night* – only two full days to produce a walking cane that would be judged by all the well-to-do eyes of Inthington. She kicked herself for being distracted by Needle overnight; every waking and sleeping hour should have been dedicated to keeping her job and that meant figuring out how, on this earth, she would assemble the walking cane without bits flying here and there. "We'll be all right, won't we?" She desperately needed her sister to say it would be so.

"Absolutely! When all is done, we can go feed the pigeons down by the square, if you like?" said her sister. "Maybe even take a trip to the sweet shop – thanks to you, we managed rent last month. Remember Landlord Hempenstall's scrunched up face when I poured the money into his hand? That stopped him and his ugly plans to get rid of us, didn't it? All going well, we might even have a few spare coins this month."

"I don't like sweets anymore," lied Glory, head down. Half a wage didn't taste so good.

Dee-Dee pinched the hanging hem of Glory's dress and sighed away the guilt that settled in her heart – no little sister of hers, no matter how ambitious she might be, should ever have to work for a living, but needs must. She threw her fingers into a bowl of flour and dragged two stripes across her own cheekbones. "Nothing is going to get in our way because I'm a warrior and that makes you one too, sis," she said, adding two more stripes for her sister's cheeks. "I'm proud of you, Gloria, and Mama and Papa would be too. One day you'll show them all – *Gloria's Glorious Emporium* – I can see your name over the door! You'll be a powerful lady." She waved her hands above Glory's head and a cloud of flour floated down.

"Thanks, Dee-Dee." Glory gave her a quick hug. As

her sister burst into a cheerful song about someone screaming for ice cream, Glory left her be.

❖

Glory closed the front door behind her and used the tip of her boot to test the pathway for black ice. It was dark and freezing out and, as she walked on, she clamped her wooden hand across her stomach for extra cover.

She skidded to a halt.

Despite the early hour, a ghostly puff of breath floated beyond a lamppost on the opposite side of the narrow road: *Landlord Hempenstall.* Sly and mean. She'd seen their landlord there before, stalking them like a vulture. He was planning their eviction, preying on their father's woodwork that decorated every corner of their home.

Standing out from the shadows, his bloodthirsty eyes glared at the house and then at Glory – a glare that clearly said it would only be a matter of time. Reaching out his grey, ungloved hand, he beckoned her, slowly, with his forefinger.

"You'll have your rent," Glory hissed and ran and ran, huffing her way through the inches of slush and driving sleet. The fluffy white beauty of recent days was gone and the streets had turned into rivers of filth. She passed a row of shops, crossed Eyelet Bridge and turned left along the riverside. Turning right onto a small lane, she arrived at the back gate of the emporium.

"Oh, Fuss… I mean, Magpie! You put my heart sideways!" With the ground a soggy mess from the melting snow, Magpie had perched on a branch that swooped across the top of the gate and had squawked a loud good morning as Glory walked in. "Is he here? Is he still inside?" Glory was surprised at how excited her words sounded.

She rushed to the door and, having left it unlocked all night, pushed it open and called out his name as she whipped off her hat. She could see the slit of light shining from the bottom of the storeroom door.

Glory entered and her heart sank.

He was gone.

Chapter Ten

Glory kicked the pole of the lamp, bouncing flashes of warning, amber light off the storeroom walls. She'd left a *stranger* alone in the emporium! Oh, how could she have been so stupid? So careless and impetuous? She could hear the words in her head, clear as day; a grown-up voice, a mix between Mrs Quick's anger and her old headmistress's disappointment. She had begged him to stay the night in there, it being so cold outside. And, because of his honest eyes and nervous smile or whatever it was, she had put all her trust in him, put *everything* at stake. All on a whim. How *could* she?

"The jewellery for the ball!" she cried. Her belly flipped and her heart suddenly raced. She marched into her workshop and flung the velvet curtain wide open.

There he was! Standing, bold as brass, in the middle of the shop floor! He was facing her, fluttering candle in hand and an awkward smile on his face.

"NEEDLE!" Glory grabbed the candle and ordered him back into the workshop. "Are you trying to have me sacked? Mrs Quick would have my guts for garters and you in jail if she found you in here." That wiped the smile from his face.

Needle gulped. He was sure there would be a friendly good morning, considering he'd done what she'd asked and stayed the night, frightened and curled up under the glassless display cabinet in the storeroom with little other than a couple of floor-cloths and dust for cover. He'd spent most of those hours counting to sixty, over and over again, waiting for the minute that she'd surely burst through that door with her great plan of how to get him home.

Unsure what would come next, he rocked from one foot to the other and hunched his shoulders as he watched her put a little bit too much care into closing the curtains.

She turned and held the candle up to his face,

frowning when she saw his nervous stance. "What's wrong with you?" She tipped his foot with hers to stop his bobbing.

"Huh?"

"You look like a bold pup who has done something he shouldn't. Did you touch anything in there?" She flicked open the curtain again and glanced towards the new cabinet, unable to see much more than a chink of reflected light here and there.

Needle whispered under his breath, "I'm still here, ain't I?"

"Oh, for goodness' sake, speak up! Well? Did you put a finger on anything in there?"

Needle put his hands on his hips, felt brave for a moment and dropped them to his side. "No, Miss Glory."

On hearing his shaking words, Glory grimaced for being so harsh. "Oh. I see. I just thought that you might have… well, needed to… *take* some of the things I made. Not that I wouldn't understand – I can see you could do with some money to, like, eat or something, but—"

"Things *you* made?" His hands were on his hips again and this time they were staying.

"Oh, Needle, do we have to do this again? Is this about Magpie? I *know* she's yours, so let's not fight over everything else. Of course those jewels are mine, I… I made them with my own hands." She glanced down at her wooden hand, now pointing angrily at Needle. She put it behind her back and sighed.

"When you first got your hands on that piece with three blue stones, it had an amber stone in the middle," said Needle as he grabbed the candle and barged back onto the shop floor. Despite being cleverly adapted to suit the emporium's customers' orders, he'd recognised his missing Christmas decorations the second he'd seen them. He pointed to a choker necklace in the centre of the display cabinet. "And as for that one, you added the band and them pearls – I only had clear sea-glass there. And this one over here, I seen that beetle-wing before…"

"*Beetle-wing?*" Glory quietly asked and gasped as he pointed at Magpie's first gift – the mysterious tear of liquid rainbow.

He stormed back into the workshop and held the candle up to her face. It was clearly blushed. "And *you* ask *me* if I've stolen anything? Less of your red talk, if you don't mind."

Glory frowned. She wasn't sure what he was implying with the red talk but understood she was being accused of stealing – that part was black and white. "I have *never* stolen anything in my life!" Glory gulped and held her bag with all its accidental beads, runaway penny and snatched cake close. "And I don't have red talk," she added, hoping he'd think she knew what it meant.

Needle heard a green, dishonest tone to her words but thought best not to question it.

She looked down at the ground. "Anyways, they were all a gift… from Magpie."

"A *stolen* gift."

For a while, they stood staring at each other in silence, until curiosity got the better of her.

"You really did make them, Needle?" She pointed towards the cabinet.

Her tone had changed colour and Needle couldn't stop the big smile that spread across his face – he had, after all, stood up for himself. He didn't bother answer and pretended, or at least that's how he began, to study Glory's impressive sketches of a walking cane.

"Are you an apprentice too, Needle? Which shop?"

"Did you draw these?" asked Needle as he nodded at the line of paper pinned to the shelf with pretty glass hairpins.

"What? Oh, those. Yes – all mine."

"Cross your heart?" he asked – after all, it was hard to believe it. These drawings were the work of a proper artist! Or a master of some sort!

Glory waved her wooden hand this way and that across her heart. "Hungry?" It was her way of checking all was forgiven. She sat down on her stool, untied her bag and offered Needle a jam roll.

Intrigued, he unfurled it into a long strip and licked the juicy red jam from the sponge and that made Glory smile. It still held heat and reminded Needle of the warm scone, the nutty bread and the cheek-sucking lemon cake Magpie had brought home. He stopped chewing for a second – was he now face-to-face with his bird's secret supplier?

"Is that what you be making next?" he asked as he nodded towards the sketches and licked his fingers.

"That's what I'm *trying* to make. You know the Millbank? The huge gallery down by Eyelet Bridge?"

"Think I seen it – the one with all them steps going up to the door? At home, they always put doors

132

on the ground where they belong." A sudden ache somewhere inside made him flinch. "My home... it *was* right there..." A confused expression grew on his face.

"Eh... yes. I see." Glory flicked a look at the bruise on his forehead. "The gallery is owned by Lord Buckram?" Pausing to see if there was even a hint of recognition on Needle's face, she continued, "He's asked Mrs Quick to make a walking cane for this inventor that's coming to Inthington. Oh, he's a great man, this Master Sharp, Needle," she cried and slapped her heart with both hands. "You do know *all* the best toys were invented by him? And really, really important machines, too, like the hairdryer. Oh, and the radio. He's even working on one with moving pictures on it – the *television*, he calls it. And the first gramophone – you know, the machine that plays music records?" She drew a circle in the air with her wooden forefinger.

Needle shrugged. What *was* she rattling on about?

"And, ooh..." She flicked a switch next to her and light beamed from her desk lamp. "Didn't he invent the lightbulb...? I *think*." She blew out the candle. "Well, he travels the world with his machines and he's coming to Lord Buckram's gallery tomorrow evening to showcase his latest work. It's a huge thing, you know, to be asked to make something for Master Sharp," she added, not convinced Needle was expressing enough amazement. "And there's a big fancy ball, a party, for him tomorrow night and every great man and woman in Inthington will be there. The best of them wearing my... *our* jewellery! Needle?"

Needle was distracted; he was astounded by her work. To take his Christmas decorations – appealing to the eye and firmly constructed by any standard – and turn them into delicate pieces of pure beauty surely required more than skill alone. "You be great... I... I mean, what you made – the jewellery – they be really good. You be sprinkling magic on them. You made my decorations into something proper." At the sound of his own blossom-pink voice, Needle silently begged his red cheeks to go away.

"I'm afraid I have you fooled, Needle. Yes, I can make things look good, but if it wasn't for Magpie's gifts – *your* gifts – they'd just fall apart thanks to *this*." She stared down at her wooden hand. "And I only have until tomorrow evening to get this... this stupid cane done." She picked up the bare stick on her desk and dropped it again. "Sure as I sit here, when Master Sharp leans on it, the top will fall to pieces and make him stumble. And it'll be all down to me and my blasted hand. Mrs Quick has already warned me, you know. One more mistake and I'm out."

Needle could feel her worry and, not sure what to do, he picked up her pencil-sharpening pocket-knife, admired its silver handle, etched much like fine lace, and flicked it closed. A shock of cold hit his palm and, as its sad story unfolded, he threw it back onto the desk. He rubbed his palm. "Um…"

He gulped when Glory launched towards the knife. She picked it up, delicately cupping the cold hard metal against her chest like he'd once done to a tiny, lost wren. He looked apologetically at her and whistled a yellow tune. The knife's story told him Glory had worries of her own and this made his own problems swell up inside. Perhaps he would have to go it alone, knowing it would be hard to find a road that led all the way to 1864.

He walked slowly towards the door. "You have a lot to do, with your stick and all. I be on my way – maybe I be finding my own way home."

"Wait. Please tell me where you come from. Tell me how you got here."

"Only if you don't say I be lying. It don't sound real, even to me own ears."

Once again, she crossed her heart. She pulled a length of hair from behind her ear and, using two fingers, began to plait it ever so neatly as she listened to every word he spoke; hunting treasures and giving them new life as he tinkered away in his trove. How he could hear their stories from the past by holding them in his palm – a skill he learned from his father. Glory held her breath when he spoke so softly about him; how he missed him and how his life back home, and that of his mother, was colourless. That cut Glory to the bone – having lost her own parents to fever only months ago, she knew what it was like to lose something that, no matter how hard you searched, could never be found. He continued his story. His sorrow faded and something else, curiosity perhaps, rose as he spoke of how he blistered his foot on a hot shard and, finally, the story of the plaque and its Great Flood.

Hard as it was, as she listened to his tale, she found herself believing.

"The pocket-knife was your da's?"

"Yes," she whispered and questioned Needle with her eyes.

"Sorry you lost your da, Glory. When I picked it up I didn't mean to listen to its story, it being private and all."

Glory nodded and gently kissed the pocket-knife. Much like the heat it once held from her father's touch, she cherished the idea that her father's story was still alive, still hot, somewhere deep inside. She offered Needle one of those smiles only two people with the same sorrow could share.

"Have you them with you, the hot shards?"

"In my satchel," he confirmed and nodded his head towards the storeroom.

Glory placed the last of her teacake into her bag and Needle watched as she tied the tassels into a perfect bow with one hand. By the second, he was becoming more impressed. He looked down at his father's boots: laces missing from one and a tangled mess on the other – the best he could do.

Glory followed Needle into the storeroom and he pulled the five cotton-wrapped pieces from his satchel. He placed them on the floor and asked Glory if she wouldn't mind twisting them around until the letters matched. He turned his attention to his satchel to pull the final square from his father's woollen sock while Glory read the list of names on the plaque.

"Oh, not on your nelly!" she cried as she read out the date of the 6th January, 1928. She scrambled to her feet and ran back to her workshop. Needle heard her curse something and that was followed by the sound of pages being flicked at great speed.

"Ah, heck!" She stomped her way back to Needle and held a book of sorts before his eyes.

"Wh... what am I looking at?"

"LOOK!" She hammered her wooden finger on the scribbled numbers at the top of the page. "5th of January! *today* is the 5th of January!"

"Whoa! The flood is happening *tomorrow*?"

Glory threw the receipt book into the sink and knelt down before the shards. "*Florence Hyde, eighteen, of Ribbon Lane*, Needle – that's only minutes from where I live. And her sister, *Doris*. Oh, she's only three! *Harry Harding, Lilian Sears*... I think her name rings a bell. And look; some poor thing just called *Unnamed, Inthington Town Jail.* This is rotten, Needle," she whispered. She silently made her way through the remaining names. She gasped. "*Mrs Fidelma Quick? My mistress!*"

"Really?" Needle waved his head left to right, following the lines of letters.

Glory was quick and not too surprised to realise that he was unable to read. She pointed to her mistress' name. "There… OH! Look at them all! They're going to DIE, Needle!" She clamped her hand across her forehead.

Needle added, urgently, "There be another piece in my—"

"Shh!" Glory froze as she counted the chimes from the clock. "It's eight o'clock already? Mrs Quick'll be here any minute. You've got to go, but please – you have to come back. After dark?"

Needle nodded.

"Wait." Glory ripped out a page from the receipt book and scrambled to find a pencil. Kneeling down, she placed the paper over the shards and, holding the pencil at an angle, rubbed its long nib back and forth across the page.

"Look at that!" said Needle, amazed to see the plaque's letters rapidly appear on the page.

Glory folded it and squeezed it into her pouch bag, instructing Needle to quickly gather the shards in the cotton. Having tucked it all back into his satchel, he was half way down the corridor when Glory pushed him to the side and marched to the back door.

"Oh! Poor Magpie, I almost forgot – her breakfast!" She looked out into the yard. Over the sound of lashing sleet that pounded the pavestones, there was a squawk. Magpie leapt from the garden chair, landed by Glory's feet and circled her boots.

"Shush! I'm here now. You must be hungry." Glory reached for her bag but Magpie flew up and pecked it from her hand. The bird flapped around Glory's head, tossing her hair with the bag's dangling tassels.

"FUSSPIE! MAGPOT! NO! That's my bag!"

Magpie dropped it from her beak on the far side of the garden gate and it fell to the slushy ground.

"How dare you! MY DOLL!" Glory cried, fearing the slush would soak through the bag. It was hard to explain the special bond she had with her ragdoll, regardless of her maturing, twelve years of age. "Needle, your bird is acting the maggot! What is the matter with you, Magpie?"

Magpie landed by the gate, spread her wings and bobbed up and down.

"Something *is* the matter. She be wanting me to follow," said Needle as he threw the strap of his satchel over his shoulder.

"The flood?" Glory guessed. "You can't stop the water but the more people that know about it..."

Needle nodded. He turned and looked at Glory, desperately wanting her to come too but he knew that asking her to do that would just earn him a snide remark. And rightly so – dropping everything and putting her livelihood at risk all for a bird's flapping wings and a stranger's hunch would be positively silly. It wasn't something you'd do on the spur of the moment. Yet...

Glory looked back towards the corridor. A light flicked on.

"Wait! My hat."

Needle raised his eyebrows.

"You're right – too late!" She shook her head like a wet dog and howled, "LET'S GO!"

Chapter Eleven

Glory and Needle sprinted after Magpie. The rain and sleet fell – the sort that fell upwards and sideways no matter which way they faced. Without stalling, they rounded the corner of the narrow lane and turned left onto the busy quay. Magpie flew across the road to the side of the River Notion and Glory followed.

Needle dashed half way across before being stunned by the sound of a honking horn.

"NOW! RUN FOR IT!" yelled Glory from beyond a mound of slush.

Whichever way Needle looked, strange horseless carriages with blinding lights cut through the curtain of sleet, chasing each other up and down the road. Even more so than the night before, when Needle had followed Magpie to the back gate of the emporium, the roads were chaotic; horseless carriages, some long as trains, people and bicycles rushing without any pattern nor manners and it was all too noisy to think. He covered his ears with his hands. The sounds were tangled together! A rotten mixture of murky brown! Wheels turned, wipers swished and smoke plumed out of pipes. When he finally made it across to Glory, he stood at the river's edge with his hands on his thighs, panting. "Why – all – the – rushing?"

"They're *motorcars*! Gosh! Is it your first time seeing them?" she asked with a burst of excitement and ignored his attempts to answer. She spun around, waving at the tall buildings, distant traffic lights, trams and boats and any modern thing she always took for granted. "Tell me what else is new to you!"

"What's *new* is that you've all forgotten how to do time properly in 1928. Rush! Rush! Rush! Your minutes be like seconds and your hours be like minutes. Why is everyone in a hurry? You must've been born late, the lot of you!"

"Come on, keep moving!" was Glory's response as she marched onwards along the low embankment wall. She pointed towards their crow.

Magpie flew from towering post to post on boats that lined the River Notion to their right. Needle's eye followed the posts' chains downwards to where they dangled angry metal claws over the frozen water. Needle frowned. Was that how schmocking was done in these strange days?

On the far side of the river, above the bare treetops, he spotted a great statue upon the pointed roof of Lord Buckram's Millbank Gallery. The statue was of a powerful woman and she overlooked all of Inthington. In her hand, she held what appeared to be a pitch-fork, threatening to pierce the underside of the darkest cloud Needle had ever seen. A squawk from Magpie moved his eyes and his legs onwards until Eyelet Bridge emerged before them. Rather than cross over it, Magpie continued along the quay.

"Wait! See that road? To the left of the gallery?" Glory pointed towards a narrow road that sloped away from the far side of the river. "*Ribbon Lane* – that's one of the roads listed on the plaque, remember? That girl, Florence, wasn't it?" Glory pulled the paper with its pencil rubbing from her bag and sheltered it from the sleet with her wooden hand. "Yes, Florence. And her little sister. Bet they live in one of the basement flats. Others are from that road too," she confirmed after checking the list again. "We have to warn them."

Glory ran to Eyelet Bridge and crossed it. Needle, having difficulty keeping up with her speed, watched her turn right onto Broidery Quay and stop to catch her breath opposite the entrance to Ribbon Lane. As Needle caught up, Magpie dived down and flapped her wings against his head.

"Leave it, Magpie!" panted Needle, "Give us a second, would you?" He waved her away only for her to do it again. He watched as she flew off towards Eyelet Bridge before turning back, more determined. In good time, he wrapped his arms around his head.

"MAGPIE! *This* is the way we're going!" Glory pointed towards Ribbon Lane. As Magpie flew off again towards the bridge, Glory grabbed Needle's satchel strap and pulled him across the road.

Opposite the sidewall of the Millbank Gallery that ran the length of Ribbon Lane, stood several four-storey houses. As they approached, Glory instructed Needle to get knocking before she disappeared down the wrought iron steps towards the first basement door.

Needle's walking immediately slowed – it wasn't a conscious slowing, it was as though every bone in his body was doing its best to stall what would come next. How could he knock on a stranger's door on his own and *talk*? Just like that?

"Cheek of the old biddy," cried Glory, "she slammed her flamin' door in my face, so she did!" She pounded along the footpath and nudged Needle to get on with it. She continued on towards a house farther down.

The nudge helped him start the climb down until he finally stood facing a black door. A rude, red-tinted word from Glory met his ears, followed by the slam of another door. With his trembling fist raised and ready to knock, the door opened and a tired, thin looking girl – no more than seventeen with a young child on her hip – appeared before him. Both Needle and the girl yelped at the same time.

"If it's pennies you're after, be off with you. We have enough mouths to fill." She closed the door and peered out the narrow window to its right.

"Miss, I need to be warnin' you," he said to the glass until it fogged up between them. He wiped it with his sleeve and she jumped backwards. "I BE WARNING

YOU!" Whether it was the fear or unexpected good luck, he was loud this time.

"WHO GOES THERE?"

Needle leapt back from the door and looked up towards the voice. A tall lady, dressed in a green overcoat and matching umbrella, stood half way up the steps to the main house and, whether it was due to the height of two flights of steps, the pelting sleet from above or her general appearance, she had a face like thunder.

"What are you doing to Miss Hyde? FLORENCE! Are you hurt?" She bent over the railing and searched for her basement neighbour.

"She *will* be hurt – worse even," spluttered Needle.

"That's it, I'm calling the police." The lady ran up the steps, fiddled with her keys and pushed open her door.

Needle stood silent for a moment, waiting for her to yell from her doorstep or, no doubt, have one of her servants run to the nearest police station, but neither happened. He shrugged and used the opportunity to run back up to the footpath.

"Well? Did you tell them?" yelled Glory from several houses down. Even from that distance, Needle could see her red cheeks, balled fist and stomping boots as she made her way towards him. Having doors slammed in her face had left its mark.

"Eh, no... you see..." attempted Needle before pointing towards the tall lady standing at the threshold of her home holding what appeared to be a candlestick to her mouth. She held another smaller piece to her ear.

"POLICE? Officer Pocket?" shrieked the woman into the candlestick.

Glory reached Needle's side and glanced up the steps. "She's on the telephone, calling the police! What the heck did you do? RUN!"

Glory dragged Needle to the top of the road. Baffled, he twisted his head back towards the houses – how on earth did that woman call a policeman by candlestick? When they reached the low wall of the River Notion and looked on towards Eyelet Bridge, Glory stopped in her tracks and ducked down onto her hands and knees. Needle crashed into her.

"Ah, sorry!" cried Needle. His offer to help her to her feet was dismissed and she stood, not bothering to straighten her skirt or rub the grit from her ripped stockings.

"Listen!" Glory pointed towards the bridge. "The police are coming!"

Needle pulled his ears out wide and heard the threatening sound of a distant siren. "This way?" he suggested. In one leap, he was over the low embankment wall.

Chapter Twelve

"We be safe here – for a while anyhows," said Needle, sounding unsure as he sat down on the pebbles beneath the first arch of Eyelet Bridge. He picked at the dirt beneath his nails as he studied the heaving river. 1928 seemed to be in a permanent hurry but the tide still switched only twice a day – like a giant, it breathed swells of salty seawater into its veins and exhaled it all out again, diluted with fresh water from inland. Right now, it was low tide. The water flowed out towards the mouth of the sea but its level was far higher than Needle expected; with his back against the arch and his legs stretched out, his boots reached the water's edge with its coat of ice, now melting and broken into jagged shapes. Each sheet bobbed along slowly but beneath the surface, the river raged.

He shivered as the jagged silver sound of ice scraping against rock on the far side of the arch hit a nerve deep in his ears, so, to distract himself, he kicked at the pebbles, throwing them up and out onto the ice.

Glory tutted. "Make yourself at home, why don't you." Her tone was definitely purple – a mix of fierce red and sad blue.

What had he done? Why was she annoyed and upset? Did he hit her with a pebble? No. All he'd done was sit down under the arch – it was always a good hiding spot when the bread-throwing bakers crossed over the bridge on their way home. Ah! That's what he'd forgotten: his manners! Mam would've clipped his ear. He laid his satchel neatly on the pebbles beside him and patted it into a rectangular shape, just like a cushion, ignoring his concern that any delicate contents inside might crack under the weight of Glory.

"Here you go," he said, apologetically.

Glory huffed, looked at the satchel, dismissed it,

and sat herself down on the pebbles and mud many inches to its right.

"THE RUDENESS!" she cried.

"I… I be sorr—"

"One look!" Glory scooped up a handful of pebbles and fired them across the sheets of ice. "ONE! They opened their doors, took one look at *this*…" She held her wooden hand before Needle's face. "One of them even laughed – *this* one…" she said, hammering her finger on a name half way down the list, "*and* she said I was potty! POTTY?

"No one would listen to me! I told them about the flood. I told them they would DIE," she exclaimed, waving the list in the air, "and what did they say? They told me to scarper – and I can tell you I was *perfectly* polite in everything I said."

Needle noticed her sideways glance and remembered the not-so-polite words he'd heard her shout *before* a door slammed.

"And the hag in the first house said my brain was made of wood! THE CHEEK!" Holding the list between her knees, she scooped up more pebbles with her wooden hand and threw one at a time into the river. "Told her she should look in the mirror," Glory added under her breath.

Though Needle wanted to say something – anything – he wasn't sure it wouldn't be met with a pebble between his eyes. He pretended to continue picking at his nails while he watched her face through his fingers. As her scrunched up mouth finally began to relax, her bottom lip wobbled. All her red was gone, thank goodness, but he knew her blue remained, even without her saying a word. He wasn't surprised; he knew what it felt like when strangers judged you by your looks or what you did or didn't say. He banged the hollow toes of his father's boots together, willing his brain to come up with something to cheer her up.

"Listen," he whispered and put a finger to his lips.

Glory froze, with pebbles balanced on her wooden hand, and listened hard. "What?"

Needle reached between them and pointed to a tiny disc of grey pressed down into the mud. He licked his finger, rubbed the disc until it shone and gently pushed down on it; the silver was so weak it relented and offered a quiet, white pop. Glory gasped.

"Listen," Needle repeated. Carefully, he pinched

its sides with his long nails and pulled, up and up, ever so slowly.

SCH-M-OCK!

It was a beautiful silver thimble, so fragile it could buckle from a feather's touch. Needle crawled to the river's edge and washed it. He stood up and placed it in his palm.

Glory's jaw dropped – he had spoken of how he could tell a treasure's story. She watched in silence as Needle closed his eyes and stuck out his chest.

"This thimble's owner be only a whippet of a thing but, *whoosh*, this girl had clout!" Needle began, waving his free hand over his head like a shooting star before placing it against the crook of his back. "She and this thimble darned socks for a living, but with every stitch she be dreaming of bigger things. One day, in church, she came to the rescue of a red-faced Lady-in-Waiting, sewing her torn sleeve up good and tight. And each perfect stitch was worth one step on the ladder until, at fifteen, she became the youngest ever Mistress of the Robes to, wait for it," he whispered, "only the King's mother herself!"

Glory squealed for the girl's success but quickly hushed as Needle paused, concentrating on the deepening story. "The girl was quiet, like a mouse, but she'd big ears – she be sewing royal secrets into every hem and cuff in that castle. Drop a stitch or a secret and she'd be out on her ear, she was warned. But she did – she dropped a secret… one that spared the life of the King's son and hung his royal traitor dead." Needle opened his eyes and placed the thimble on Glory's smallest wooden finger. "She said little else after she'd told the secret, afraid her own would escape; turns out she tore that Lady-in-Waiting's sleeve herself. I'd like to have a cup of tea with her," he smiled.

"Amazing!"

"It be older than you think. Happened two hundred years ago, at least."

"Again! Again! Do it again!" cried Glory. She made efforts to get up.

Needle grabbed her wooden hand. "WAIT!" From her palm, still full of pebbles, he plucked an old crooked coin.

"Ah, this be hot! Ouchy!" he pretended. "Cold ones be from the past so this be from the future." He peeped through one eye and watched her as she stared at the rusty coin. "It belonged to – *will* belong to – a kind, red-head of a lady from Inthington. She be so rich she

156

be throwin' coins in the air as she walks and this one here will land in the river. She be the richest woman in the world, all because she be making jewellery in her shop where the Queen visits every single day." He thought maybe it was best to stop there. "True story," he added when he heard her gasp.

"Do you think… could it be—"

"Anything be possible, so it is – me Mam told me that," said Needle. He frowned; in his attempt to raise her hopes, he felt his own plummet. "Mam wouldn't lie, but I now be thinking getting home from the future is one thing that *ain't* possible." He looked at Glory, desperately wanting her to say his answer was so very wrong.

Glory blinked three times, it being all she could offer, and noticed how his fingers began to tremble. "Show me how you do it, then. The treasure reading." She rummaged in the pebbles and urged him to do the same in the hope that his fingers would calm. She picked up a piece of white china. "Pretty!" she said as she wiped its surface, revealing painted blue flowers.

"Put it in your palm."

"Like this?"

"Yeah, you can wrap your fingers around it if you like. It be so cold it hurts but that be what tells you its age – the colder, the older."

"I suppose it's a bit cold," Glory offered, not sure she was feeling what she should.

"You have to *really* feel it, like think of nothing else and it'll get colder."

"Right. Yes, I see, *very* cold," she lied.

"Now close your eyes and listen." Glory did as she was told. "Not just with your ears – listen with everything; your ears, your nose, your eyes, even your heart and every bit of your thinking."

"I can't listen with my nose, what are you on about?" She looked at Needle and scowled.

"Don't be giving up. You be needing to *clear your mind*," said Needle, proud that he'd recalled his mother's words. Glory scrunched up her nose and squeezed her eyes shut. Needle watched her face turn red. "You *can* breathe though," he warned with a slap to her back, "*Breathe*!"

Glory gave up and a choice word blew out with her held breath. She fired the china back onto the pebbles. "That's stupid." She turned her attention to folding the list of lost souls.

"You should stop your rushing, Glory," Needle suggested, "Besides, all things be hard before they be easy." He searched for the china and picked it up. "Why do you let yourself talk so red all the time?" he added under his breath.

Glory's furled eyebrows reminded him that hearing colours was one of his 'special things' too. "Words have colours," he explained. "Not just the word itself, but how it be said. *Thimble* be a fingernail-pink word, all floaty with soft edges, but say it like you hate it and my head fills with red. Even the air around me. It don't be lasting long though."

"Gosh." Glory relaxed her shoulders and clasped her arms around her knees.

"There be a hundred colours because there be a hundred feelings. Happiness be yellow, fear be orange. Watch out for green words – that's when someone be lying to your face. As for blue, well that goes without saying…"

"Sadness."

Needle nodded. "Words with no colour be the saddest of them all – *empty* sad. And that's what Mam's words were when I last saw her – she was missing my da and then I go and leave, so I can't imagine what colour she be now." Glory leaned closer and rubbed his arm.

"MAGPIE! Where you been?" Needle jumped to his feet and slipped the coin, thimble and china into his satchel. He held out his arm.

Magpie declined his offer of a resting spot and landed before them, squawking and flapping her wings. She edged closer to Glory.

"Does she be limping?"

Glory reached for her. "What's wrong, little pet?" Before she made contact, the crow ducked and swiped the folded list from her lap. She flew out of the arch and landed many yards away before squawking some more.

"MAGPIE! NEEDLE, the list!"

Needle's launch at the bird urged it to fly away, list in beak. Scrambling back onto Broidery Quay, Needle and Glory gave chase, zig-zagging their way past huddled gossipers with nothing else but Master Sharp on their lips. They scurried across Eyelet Bridge and turned right, cursing their bird until the smooth road surface gave way to broken cobbles and silence.

A familiar, black-as-soot building stood before them: the town jail, as dark and cold a building now, as it was then. It brought the road to a sudden end and the right side of the building formed a sky-high wall to the river itself. Magpie flew out over the river, swooped left, flew towards the wall and disappeared.

"Magpie? Where you be?" Needle wiped the rain from his face and stepped up to the edge of the road. He looked down over the shifting ice and rushing water below. The sleet had given way to proper rain drops as they pelted down and smashed against the bobbing sheets of ice on the river. He craned his neck and looked left, up along the jail's wall.

"Get back, Needle!" Glory hooked his coat with her wooden hand. "You'll fall in!"

Needle twisted himself free and leaned further over the edge. "She flew into one of them holes in the wall, I be sure of it!"

"They're windows and you don't want to follow her – that's a jail for goodness' sake. We don't need the list – we have the shards. Step back! NOW!"

"But why has she brought us here?" He grabbed Glory's left hand, squeezed it tight and bent the top half of his body over the edge. He looked up and down the wall for any sign of his crow.

"Ouch! Your hand, it's so cold!" cried Glory – like

a snowball held for too long, this was a cold that hurt and it made Glory think of the shock of cold that Needle spoke of when he held treasures from the past.

"Just one more sec... there she be! I be seein' her tail feathers," he said as he twisted his head down and to the left. "Second window, first row. Below the level of the road." He stepped back and pushed up his soggy sleeves.

Glory shook her hand to bring heat back into it and frowned. "Don't even think about it, Needle Luckett! There's too much of a drop down to the water and not a brick to cling on to on that wall. You'll fall in."

Through the pelting rain, they heard Magpie's squawk. It sounded hollow, as though she were stuck down a well. Needle and Glory stared at each other.

"Oh!" Glory covered her mouth. "She's in trouble! You have to save her! Oh, my poor Fusspot... Magpie!"

They heard it again. This time her sound was muffled. Needle gasped. It wasn't red! It wasn't orange! It was yellow – a joyous yellow! He kicked off his left boot and pulled desperately at the laces on the other until they slackened. Throwing them and his one sock off to the side, he cried, "My girl is happy, Glory! I never heard her so yellow! Listen!" He held the flaps of his ears out and willed his crow to squawk again. He lay down on his stomach and shimmied his legs over the edge until he was out of sight.

Glory crawled to the edge of the road and peered over. Her nail-chewing, softly spoken friend, with all his stuttering and bobbing, may have been hiding some courage all along – Needle was clinging to the slippery wall with little else to grasp but cracks and tufts of feathery slime. Above the creaking sheets of ice that slapped against the black wall below, she heard him whispering to his feet and hands, telling them not to worry and where to go.

"Wait! Wait for me!" She pulled her shawl from her shoulders, wrapped it tight around her skirt and scolded herself for what she was about to do. "WHAT NOW?" Glory's body dangled from the edge and her hand and tips of her wooden fingers struggled to keep hold of the slippery cobbles above.

Needle looked up. "WHAT ARE YOU AT?" he roared, exasperated. He had enough on his plate without having her fall on top of him and he wondered was there anything this girl did without thinking things through? "Put your foot that way, three boots over and up a block."

"Left or right foot? QUICK!"

"Your heart's side."

Glory wisely moved her right foot, recalling Needle wrongly cross that side of his chest earlier. With Needle's guidance, both panned their way across the face of the wall until they stood side-by-side and peered into the narrow rectangular crevice that formed a prisoner's window. Halfway in, they could see five thick black bars – the damp list wrapped around one – but no sign of their feathered friend. They each grabbed a bar and huddled closer together and Needle swung his arm around Glory's waist for added support.

"Call her," whispered Glory.

Needle whistled gently.

Out of the darkness, a large hand shot through the bars and grabbed Glory's wrist.

"AGH!" Glory's feet slipped and Needle held her tight. The hand tightened its grip around her wrist until she found her footing. "LET ME GO!" she yelled as she knocked the man's hand, time and again, with her wooden fist. She cried out in pain with her twisted skin, her elbow scratching the stone sill and the icy coldness of the hand. She didn't know which hurt most.

Needle grappled with her wooden hand to make some room and, once out of the way, grabbed the man's fingers and began to peel them off Glory's wrist. As soon as they made contact, Needle felt it: icy cold skin against icy cold skin, as cold as the story-filled treasures he fished from the shore. All the fingers relaxed and Needle and Glory were faced with a large open palm – a palm that, by the early morning light, most definitely held the scar of a square-shaped burn.

"Needle?" A voice, weak but so warm and amber, came from the darkness.

"Da?"

Chapter Thirteen

"Oh, Needle, Needle, Needle…" The sound that came out of the dark jail cell grew warmer and brighter with each word.

Needle was glad of the lashing rain that hid the tears rolling down his face. He couldn't answer – he did try, but every hint of a word repeated itself over and over again.

"It's all right, Needle," whispered Glory. "Take a big breath." She patted his shoulder ever so gently with her heavy hand. "Mr Luckett, we can't see you. Come closer."

They heard the sound of something wooden being pulled across a stone floor and a haggard, yet smiling face appeared against the bars.

"I knew you'd come. I knew she'd bring you."

Needle's father turned his head to the side and whistled. Magpie flew up from the floor of the cell and settled on his shoulder. He kissed her gently on the head. "Your mam, Needle? Is she all right?"

Needle forced a smile and nodded, not wanting to explain how her world was colourless. "You be locked up, Da! What happened?"

"It's a long story, Needle, and one that's not so... so straight forward." He discreetly dipped his head in Glory's direction.

"You can tell her, Da. We be... friends..." He'd never had reason to say that about anyone before. He raised both eyebrows as he stared into her freckled face, seeking agreement, "and she knows where we be from."

Glory quickly nodded.

"She does? Really? Well, I had just, eh, *arrived* and couldn't quite believe my eyes, as you can imagine, so I turned back to get my bag, you see, so I could explore for a while. I climbed back up Eyelet Bridge—"

"The gap, third arch in?"

"Yes, I had just climbed back into it when the police turned up – my *hideout*, they called it."

"That be why they blocked it up with bricks."

"They said I was planning a heist. A heist! Some great inventor's invention, so they say…"

"Master Sharp?" offered Glory.

"That's the man. You found the hot treasure then? Did you, Needle? In my bag?"

Needle nodded. "The square shard? I have it here, Da." He pulled up his satchel so that it sat neatly in the gap between them and pulled out his father's woollen sock. "In here – and I found more… all of it."

"Of course you did." He reached out as far as the bars would allow and ruffled Needle's hair.

"It's a plaque, Mr Luckett," explained Glory, as she unfolded the list. "I read it with my own eyes – here's a rubbing of it; it names the people who will drown in a flood—"

"NO! That explains what I felt when I held the hot metal."

"And it's going to happen right here – *tomorrow*. I even saw my mistress' name on it."

"You did? So, you're not from the past, young lady? I thought maybe you came with—"

"Oh, sorry, Mr Luckett. I'm Gloria Bobbin." She offered her wooden hand as far in through the bars as its bulk would allow. "Call me Glory."

Mr Luckett gasped and fell backwards into his cell.

"Da!" yelled Needle as he pulled back Glory's hand.

"Well, that's no way to greet me. What was I to do, Needle? I could hardly let go and shake with my other hand now, could I?"

Needle knew that his father's odd reaction was not down to her hand – greeting someone with a missing finger or more was a daily occurrence in his line of construction work. Knocking down and building up often had its consequences. His father soon reappeared at the window and pointed at the sock that held his square shard.

"Glory, you did read the plaque, yes? All the names?" asked Mr Luckett. He was speaking urgently now. Needle gasped at the troubling dark tone of his voice; his father rarely spoke so blue and so orange all at once.

"Yes, I did."

"And my square piece? In the sock?"

"No, Da, never got to show her that bit," interrupted Needle. Glory twisted the list around to face Needle's father and pointed at the empty square to its bottom left. "We had to go – Glory's mistress was—"

"Needle. You listen now," he warned and turned

his head as angry shouts came from the far side of his cell. "It's time to use your courage, Needle – the courage you use when you climb and the courage you use when you make treasure from muddy scraps." He reached out, wrapped his hand around the back of Needle's neck and pulled him close. "Use that fight in you and shout to the world about this deadly flood. You must warn them," he ordered, "and when you've done that, you go home, do you hear?" He grabbed the sock and shook it until its contents fell out. "You have what it takes, Needle," he said and turned towards the anger that rose from behind. "Both of you – get away from here. GO!"

Gates clanged, people scuffled and he was gone.

Magpie hopped through the bars and flew out over the river, whipping their faces as she fled. She stalled up high and flapped her wings furiously. The sound of her sharp, orange cries slapped off the jail walls.

"Danger!" interpreted Needle, "We be in danger!"

"*Big* danger. Look," said Glory. She was staring at the shard that fell from the sock and, as clear as day in its etched letters, it held the words: *Gloria Bobbin*.

Needle quickly picked up the piece with his father's sock and looked at the jumble of letters before shoving it and the list into his satchel. He could guess what those letters spelled and he knew one thing – this wretched flood was now far too close to home.

"And, Needle, your papa… is he the prisoner that's on the plaque too?" Glory uttered the words she didn't want to say so quietly she wasn't sure he could even hear.

"Over there!" Needle pointed across the river towards the bridge. A boat was crashing through the ice-covered water and a streak of torchlight pierced through the downpour until it found Needle's eyes.

A voice hit them in waves; "This is Chief Officer Pocket of the Inthington Police. Halt where you are. Drop your weapons."

Needle grabbed Glory's wooden hand. "To the road, Glory, go that way!"

They scaled the wall, heading up and to the left towards the road. It was no more than a wide step away when Glory placed her foot into the last window and a fat hand reached out from inside and grabbed her bootlaces. The policeman's torch, now beaming from directly below, flicked from one to the other as she kicked and screamed. Rainwater poured down the face of the wall and splashed into her eyes.

Without a free hand to wipe it away, she blinked and kicked and slipped.

"GLORY!"

She landed with a smash onto one large sheet of ice just to the side of the boat. The ice dipped below the surface, taking her with it, and rose back up again throwing her off to one side. Needle watched as she grappled with the ice.

Without having to tell them where to go, Needle's feet and hands raced downwards. He didn't take his eyes off Glory. A hook on the end of a wooden pole swung out from the boat and grabbed her right arm, enough to hold her head above water.

"I BE COMING!"

"NO! NO! GO!" Her words were choked and spluttered. She spoke again, words Needle could not work out. They were the palest of pale blue.

Her head tilted to one side and her eyes closed.

Chapter Fourteen

Had it been daytime, Needle reckoned he'd have been able to see Inthington's clocktower from where he sat. It was newly built back home and he was glad it was still there sixty-four years on. He pulled his ears wide on hearing its chime, and counted.

"It be midnight, Da," he whispered through the jail bars.

His father's thin arm squeezed through the bars and ruffled Needle's hair. "Time flies, son." One hour together hardly scratched the surface of the time they'd been apart. "Now, when you're ready."

"Sorry, here it be." From his satchel, Needle pulled his father's wooden box of favourite finds, rescued from his damp bag in the chamber over the third arch of Eyelet Bridge. He placed it down on his side of the jail bars. Not unlike Magpie, Needle stretched out one cramped leg, wriggling it above the River Notion before tucking in back into the windowsill. Only having enough room to fold himself like a slice of batch loaf didn't matter – to be alongside his father was all the comfort he needed right now.

"The reason I keep this box of treasures in my bag is so that I can travel, Needle. When we hold each piece, we can feel its story – its *history*. That part you know well, but keep it in mind. Now, show me your hag stone, son."

Needle pulled the stone through his collar and held it towards his father. He licked his finger and wiped it. "You might see another world when you look through it – I know that bit too, Da."

"Yes. But, instead of *looking* through it, imagine if you were to *go through* the hole, Needle. Do you know what would happen? Not only might you see another world, you might be in it too."

Needle scratched his head despite there being no itch. It was hard enough squeezing himself onto the jail windowsill, let alone squeeze through the tiny hole in his hag stone. To be sure, he pushed the tip of his little finger through the hole as far as it would go.

"The gap over the third arch on Eyelet Bridge…
it's not like the gap into our trove. It's different. It's a
hag stone – a giant one."

Needle's mind flew back to how its smooth edges
surprised him when he was chasing his thief of a
bird. The edges were curved! Of course it was a hag
stone! Now that he knew it, it could never have been
anything else.

"When I first met Magpie, she would fly to me
from that gap over the third arch just as soon as I set
foot on the pebbles."

"I remember that," said Needle.

"That's where she'd built her nest – in the gap over
the third arch. Soon as we fixed up our trove over the
second arch, it didn't take long for her to move in.
Remember building her nest?"

Needle nodded as Magpie hopped up to the
windowsill from the cell floor and sat between them,
preening her feathers as she would often do when
people spoke of her.

"One day, there was no sign of her. I went about
my work, searching for building jobs. It wasn't my
day for luck of that sort so, on my way home, I hunted
for treasure. I needed to find something to sell, you

see, and soon. That's when I found the marble that's now in my box." He slid out its lid and tapped the green marble. "It wasn't a lot but, considering I didn't have Magpie's help, it was a start. When I reached Eyelet Bridge there was still no sign of her." He shook his head and looked at Needle. "I was worried. Worried for our friend and worried I wouldn't have her help to find things in the mud. So I climbed into the hag stone gap, hoping to find her asleep in her old nest."

"Did you find her?"

"No. It was dark in there so I rummaged in my bag for matches. I held the marble in my hand and, of course, I felt its story begin. You know the one – with the little boy and the marble race?"

"They made a track in the field for the marbles to roll in. That be where he found a chalice."

"And that's where I ended up. One sunny day, in 1775, I climbed out of the gap and, not five minutes south of here, I was stood in *that* field. I had travelled back in time, Needle. And I've done it many a time since, using the treasures in this here box." He waved both hands over the box as though it was the glowing hearth of his home.

Needle gasped. "You can travel anywhere?"

"Not any*where*, any *time*. And not just me – anyone who has learned to read treasures' stories can do it once they are through the hag stone. Even Magpie, so it seems."

Needle nodded, then gulped. "Da! I think I did it myself! Just before I arrived here, I went through the hag stone and I listened to the marble's story and, when I was done, I be feelin' all hot. And didn't one of them floating seeds land on me! A summer seed, Da, in *winter*?" He shook his head in disbelief: he'd travelled to 1775 and hadn't even known it!

His father smiled. "And that's how you travelled here: you held the hot shard when you'd passed through the hag stone. Of course, the plaque with its story of flooding won't be made until sometime after tomorrow – that's why the shards still hold heat now. You can travel to the time of any treasure's story, be it a year or three hundred years old. You'll arrive in the same place though – wherever the hag stone is. Needle, you wouldn't believe how things were so different in the past."

Needle thought of all the strange and wonderful treasures his father brought home, day after day – all shiny, almost as new. "Is that where you found the fine things for Mam to sell? In the past?"

Needle's father nodded and, with a sigh loaded with regret, explained that some treasures may not have been *beneath* the mud waiting for him to find, but he always did his best to leave something interesting from 1864 in their place. Needs sometimes must.

"YOU CAME HOME!"

Needle's father placed a hand over Needle's mouth. "Quiet, son."

"You came home, didn't you? Every time. How did you do it, Da? Can we do it? Can we go back to Mam?"

Needle's father fished around in the contents of the box and plucked out the wooden drawer handle. "This is what I used to get home. I'd hold it as soon as I'd return to the hag stone and listen to its story. It mightn't look like much but it's real treasure – it holds all the history of our home that we need. When I travelled to the past, this handle was hot to touch because it was from the future, just like the shards. I suppose that's why I was shocked to find the hot square piece. The handle's cold now, of course, it being from the past."

He placed the handle into Needle's open palm, cupping his own hand over the top. They silently waited while the shock of cold made its presence known.

"I see her," whispered Needle. Three of them sitting around the kitchen table before empty plates almost entirely licked clean. Mam singing at the top of her voice a song about home, sweet home, grabbing both their hands and swaying side to side. When she was done, she winked and squeezed their hands three times: I-love-you. Now, sixty-four years later, Needle could feel the triple pulse of his father's fingers over his – he'd felt his mother's message too.

"It's time to go back, Needle," said his father. "Glory has been warned about the flood and you've done all you can do. It's not safe here. Take this treasure, go through the hag stone. Go home." He clamped Needle's fingers around the drawer handle.

There was no doubt Needle wanted to go home. Oh, to be with Mam! But leave Da behind? Leave Glory and all the other souls to drown, to *die*? Most likely Da, too? Going home was not the right answer. It was wrong. *Da* was wrong. But he couldn't quite find the words to tell him. Instead, he froze like a statue.

"Needle."

Needle managed to shake his head. It never worked at home when he was being told to go to bed too early, but it was all he could do right now.

"I'm telling you to go. NOW." Needle could sense a sudden redness in his father's voice.

"Not without you, Da." His voice was barely there.

"I'm staying here. I want to stay here. When they realise I never wanted that invention, they'll show me the door and I'll be free. Free to explore this land. I don't want to go home."

Clearly his father was lying, but his tell-tale green words were swimming in blue – much like his teary eyes.

Needle placed the handle back in the box and returned it all to his satchel. "Come on, Magpie." Swinging his legs out, he twisted onto his stomach and found footholds for both feet. "It be time to go back to the gap. Bye, Da," said Needle, with three gentle squeezes of his father's thumb.

Chapter Fifteen

"That's it. I'm calling for Dr Johnston again."

"Dee-Dee, please, please listen to me. It's all true, every bit of it. The flood – it *will* happen." Glory used all her energy to sit up in her bed. "THEY'RE GOING TO DIE! *I'M* – GOING – TO –" Glory's voice, punctuated by sharp breaths, stuttered to a halt as she fought back tears.

"Gloria, I have no idea what's come over you, but whatever was in that river water has messed up your thinking." Dee-Dee lay her sister back down, tucking her matted curls against the pillow, just as their mother would do. "Look at you! Half asleep and rabbiting on about some flood and finding needles and plaques and whatnot. I've told you, you're safe now. And it was only *you* that fell, no one else. *No one drowned.*"

"*Needle*, Dee-Dee? That's the boy. Where is he?" Glory swung her aching legs out of the bed and attempted to stand.

"Over my dead body – you stay put." Less patiently second time around, Dee-Dee lay Glory down and pulled the bed sheets right up under her chin. "If you are referring to that beggar boy – you should've known better. Officer Pocket says he was playing tricks on you, getting your help to free a criminal. Really, Gloria, must you always be so reckless? How many times do we have to tell you to think before you act? And *speak*, for that matter – you shouldn't have called Officer Pocket that rude name." Dee-Dee shook her head in disappointment but swiftly followed it with a sympathetic smile. "That boy's gone now so you're safe. You don't need to worry yourself about him. No doubt it won't be long before he's behind bars too."

"But, Dee-Dee…" Glory's tears came.

"GLORIA GERALDINE BOBBIN! What's with the tears?" She pinched Glory's nose in an attempt to cheer her up. "This whole thing has shook you to the bone, hasn't it?" Dee-Dee placed her palms on Glory's cheeks and took a long, worried breath – tears from Glory were most certainly a rare thing. "You need more rest, I think, and a good dose of patience – that's all," she reassured her sixteen-year-old self, wishing she could check with her mother if she was handling all this the right way. "Try to sleep. I'm only downstairs in the kitchen if you need me." Before she rose, she smacked flour from the flapping legs of her oversized tweed trousers. "I'm way behind on my order for today's delivery, with the ball being only hours away, and I still have to—"

Glory bolted upright. "WHAT?" She grabbed her pounding forehead and slapped her sister's thigh with her wooden hand. "You weren't wearing those this morning… unless… NO! NO! NO! How AWFUL!"

"I beg your—"

"What day is it? What time is it?" She saw the chain of her father's pocket-watch on her bedside table and pulled it out from beneath her soggy ragdoll, emporium key and scattering of beads that had been emptied from her pouch bag. She flicked it open. Her eyes shot to the window: *daylight*. Dull as it was, it was very much daytime daylight as it slid beneath her heavy curtain. She'd slept through the night and most of the day! *The day of the flood!* Time had slipped away – time she should have used to shout and warn from the rooftops.

She needed an excuse to get out.

"I have to go! The walking cane! It's for tonight and I haven't even started it!"

"You're not going anywhere, stick or no stick." Pausing at Glory's mirror, Dee-Dee adjusted her short tie and used her palm to press a wave of skilfully curled hair against her forehead. "Mrs Quick will have to make her own stick. Serves her right, don't you think?"

"But… but… my job, Dee-Dee! Mrs Quick will have me sacked. And she won't stop there. She'll have—"

"Now, now, Gloria." Her hands were on her hips.

"And what about Landlord Hempenstall? He's out there day and night you know, waiting, and if we miss one—"

Much like the outfit she wore, Dee-Dee's voice was powerful. "*Gloria.*"

She didn't need to say anything more. Glory lay down flat. Dee-Dee grabbed her tea-towel from the end of the bed, blew her a kiss and went back down the stairs.

On hearing the creak from the third step, Glory threw back her covers and pulled across her blue embroidered curtain. Every colourful motif on it was lovingly stitched by her own hand over many months and, when closed, it read like a picture-filled storybook. In contrast to its rainbow of colours, icy cold rain poured against the window, carried in waves by the wind. The morning, and everything in sight, was the dullest of greys.

Her head spun; too much sleep and too much river water. She needed to think, and think fast and not doing so could cost her her life, not to mention the lives of thirteen others.

"Save my life. Save their lives. Save my job. Save Dee-Dee's job." She breathed four foggy patches onto the window, hoping saying it all out loud would tell her what to do. "But how? *HOW?*" she cried. Her heart raced, her skin itched. She grabbed her throat to rub away what could only have been a scream that was telling her to *start somewhere*. She opened the window, closed her eyes and sucked in several deep breaths of fresh air. Between each breath, a whisper was carried on the wind. Quiet, at first, and then louder.

"Go up three, across two. Foot now, push up."

Glory's eyes shot open. A head of soggy hair with bits of twigs rose up from the bottom of the window and two blinking eyes with spidery wet lashes peered in. Despite not knowing which of her worries to worry about first, within a split second of seeing his face, a sudden gush of joy both surprised and overwhelmed her. She wasn't about to face whatever battles that lay ahead alone.

"Needle!" Glory knelt down and, using her palm, cleared the fog from the glass between them. He smiled a shivering smile.

"Look at you. Get in! You're soaked." Glory swung open the window as far as it would go, stood back and waited. "IN!" She grabbed the neck of his shirt and, later, his rope belt to guide him in. He fell to the floor with a thud.

Needle closed his lips to soften the sound of his rattling teeth and smiled with his eyes instead. He felt warmer already now that he had found her again.

Glory's bare feet slapped across the floorboards

and she dragged her dressing table chair to the window.

"GLORIA BOBBIN, what are you at?" A shout came from the creaking third step of the stairs.

Needle shot a look at Glory. "Who that be?" he whispered.

"Shh!" Glory instructed and mouthed that it was her big sister. "I'm just getting my curtain down, Dee-Dee. Going to do a bit of sewing on it, that's all. While I rest."

There was a muffled noise and, after a few seconds, the busy sound of pots and pans and high-pitched singing rose from the kitchen. Glory hopped onto the chair and unhooked the curtain hanging on the right side.

"It's the warmest thing in here. It'll do you good." She wrapped the heavy material around Needle where he sat on the floor and knelt before him. "You're in trouble, Needle – the police have put a price on your head."

Needle had never seen a material so stunning, almost regal. He straightened his shoulders and held out his arms to study the curtain's swirling silky threads. Trees and birds, tiny figures and playful animals. Castles and clouds, shoes and hats. It was a thing of beauty. He knew it was her work, having seen such perfection before in her sketches back at the emporium. He looked up, dug his boots into the floor and spun on the spot. Wooden figurines and minuscule furniture, each no doubt carved by her father's pocket-knife, stood to attention on a picture rail. Below it, hung sketch after sketch hiding every inch of wallpaper, some framed with acorns and ivy carved from wood. As he turned, he warmed. The shivering stopped and he stood up.

Glory stood too, suddenly embarrassed by her prettier-than-needed nightgown and bare legs sticking out from its frilly hem. She discreetly hid her green ragdoll under her pillow and turned to swing open her wardrobe. "How'd you find me?" Her words were loaded with so much gratitude and relief that she wondered if he could tell by their colour.

Needle opened his satchel and removed the list of lost souls. "Say hello, Magpie," he whispered and nodded his head towards Glory. Magpie flew up and out of her snug woollen sock nest and sat briefly on Needle's shoulder before hopping over to Glory's bed.

"NO, Magpie! Off! OFF!" Glory grabbed her by the wing, wincing when one feather detached and floated slowly to the ground. Magpie froze on Glory's pillow, staring at her with one eye.

There were footsteps on the stairs. "Gloria?"

Glory raised a finger to her mouth. "Just… just sat on a pin!" she replied and waited to see if that did the job. She caught Needle's eye. "*What?* When a bird flies into a house it's a sign of death. *Death!*" she whispered as loudly as possible. "And if one lands on your bed, well that confirms it… what hope do I have?" She waved the list in his face.

189

Neither boy nor bird flinched. The silence hit her worse than any telling off she could have expected. When her breathing finally slowed, guilt hit her hard between the eyes. "Oh, I *am* sorry, Magpie." She retrieved the feather and made awkward attempts to offer it back. "I'm just not sure I can handle any more bad luck."

Tempted to grab the feather from her, Needle resisted and took it gently, having noticed her outburst was orange rather than red. "Magpie did not *fly* into the house, she was carried; that be the opposite and means good luck, not bad."

"Oh!" Glory reached over and rubbed Magpie's tail feathers with a finger. Accepting her gesture, Magpie loosened her stiff feathers, stretched out one leg and tucked it back up under her belly.

"All is good," Needle translated and started when he heard a crash of something ceramic on ceramic downstairs. "I don't want to get you into trouble. I should go."

"*We* should go."

"It be best you stay put..." Needle bit his lip. He wanted to ask her how she was so brave, so brazen. He'd never met anyone quite like her, who, rightly or wrongly, could just do what they wanted to do. Ifs and buts, and anything anyone could say, would not hold her back.

"There's no question of me staying," she said as she grabbed the first thing her hand fell on in her wardrobe. "There's more than me to save out there, Needle." Thinking of his father, she turned and gave him a pitiful look and rubbed his shoulder.

Needle scrunched up his toes and flinched. He'd disobeyed his father's order to go home overnight and instead, for each of the fourteen souls, he'd chosen a small pebble from the foreshore. In the dark of night, he'd lined them up on the embankment wall, each one different from the next – *unique*, as his mother had said. He squeezed them into the toes of his big boots, seven in each, so he could carry the weight of their death around with him lest he ever forget what was to be done. Those pebbles, *those lives*, just couldn't be lost for ever. And with every pinch and buff they gave his toes, he'd be reminded of that.

Glory pulled a heavy green and blue checked dress from its hanger and threw it over her head. The nightgown underneath would help keep her warm and, she hoped, dry. As she sat down to pull on her stockings and boots, Needle kept his head down. He thought of the letters of Glory's name etched out on the square shard like a miniature headstone and busied himself by sharpening his fingernail which had become less pointed from all the climbing.

"Did you see it? My name on the shard?"

"I seen the letters. Have it here." He pulled the curtain from his shoulders, put it on the bed and tapped his satchel.

"What about your papa? Do you suppose that's him on the shards then? The unnamed prisoner?"

"Eh, dunno," replied Needle, as he scrunched his toes again. His voice wobbled, and it didn't go unnoticed. He blushed so badly he tried to hide it with his hands.

Glory, pretending she hadn't seen, quickly stood up and peered out the window. Streams of rainwater raced along the sides of the road, pooling at overflowing drains. She followed the flow of water, looking as far to the right as her nose would allow and, as the glass fogged with her breath, two headlights trundled around the corner and came to a stop directly outside her house. Someone stepped out. They were hidden beneath their coat, held high above their head.

Three loud knocks echoed through the hall.

Glory gasped. "Three knocks? KNOCK AGAIN!" She raced out of her room and down the stairs. To her, this was a life-or-death situation, given that three knocks on a door was a sure sign of death. She barged past Dee-Dee, flattening her against the wall of the narrow hallway. She pulled open the door, screaming at the knocker to knock again.

"Gloria Bobbin," a voice greeted her. Glory's name had never sounded so revolting.

At the top of the stairs, Needle covered his ears. "Putrid red," he whispered and retreated to the safety of Glory's bedroom.

Glory gulped. "Mrs Quick."

Chapter Sixteen

"Of course your walking cane is not ready. Gloria is not well," said Dee-Dee. She leaned across the one corner of kitchen table she'd hastily cleared of sugared-lemon butterfly decorations and rubbed her sister's arm. She added, in a hushed voice, "Isn't that plain to see?"

Glory followed Mrs Quick's beady glare and looked down upon her own dress. It was inside-out.

Mrs Quick sniffed the milk that Dee-Dee had poured into their last remaining fine china jug and wrinkled her nose. "What *is* plain to see is that your delinquent sister has been liaising with wanted criminals." She pushed away her steaming cup of tea. "This beggar boy of hers was seen breaking into my shop last night. And, despite what Officer

Pocket might have to say, that makes *her* his accomplice."

Glory gasped. "No, he didn't! Needle isn't a thief. I know he's not." She wanted to defend him more by adding that he'd spent the night of his arrival there without as much as a bead taken but she was in enough trouble as it was.

Dee-Dee squeezed Glory's arm. "He's a criminal, Gloria, a clever one. I told you – it was his plan all along. He had you fooled." Dee-Dee turned to face their unexpected guest. "Gloria wasn't to know." She hastily picked up the jug of perfectly fresh milk, poured an uninvited drop into Mrs Quick's tea and pushed the cup so close to their guest its heat must have warmed her chin.

Glory looked from Mrs Quick to Dee-Dee. "You're wrong, both of you. You have to be. Needle just wouldn't do…"

Mrs Quick dragged air through her nostrils in what appeared to be a rare attempt to calm her temper, and pulled something from her purse. She dangled it in the air with the tips of her red-painted fingernails before allowing it to drop into her tea. "Snagged on one of my many glass knobs – half way up the wall of drawers, apparently. Seems your poor beggar set his sights too high."

Glory gulped. There was no mistaking it, with its layer of crusty mud and frayed ends. "Needle's bootlace," Glory whispered.

Mrs Quick grabbed her apprentice's arm and, with each word, she shook it. "Every bead, every gem, every SCRAP OF ANYTHING he stole from me will be returned to the emporium. DO YOU HEAR ME?"

"S…sorry. I really didn't think he—"

"Save your apologies for later, you STUPID girl…"

Dee-Dee rose to her feet, sending splashes of tea across the table. "Mrs Quick!"

"You shall return to the emporium with me RIGHT NOW and make my cane. *Then* I shall decide what to do with you." Mrs Quick closed her purse and straightened her hat.

Glory looked down at her lap. How could she have been so gullible? So impetuous, as always? She never gave herself the time – the patience – to think before she acted. Now that she did think about it, wasn't it easier to believe Mrs Quick's tale of being burgled than Needle's wild story of arriving from the past and foretelling a great flood? She expected the feeling of relief to wash over her – *no flood* – but, instead, she felt breathless, like she was drowning.

Glory quietly nodded at her sister that it was time to go with Mrs Quick. She stood up, and, to avoid Mrs Quick's wicked eyes, looked out through the kitchen window. Something next to their cherry-blossom tree caught her eye; in the lashings of rain, a flying bundle of black and green rose up and down before her.

Ragdoll! In Magpie's beak! The crow's message was clear as day: the ragdoll was every shade of green and, according to what Needle told her under the bridge,

green meant someone was lying through their yellow teeth.

"YOU'RE A LIAR, MRS QUICK!" Glory leaned across the table, hooked Needle's bootlace from the tea with her wooden finger and swished it and all its sloppiness across Mrs Quick's silk dress. In an attempt to catch it, Mrs Quick snagged her dress with a fingernail, pulling the silk threads into a hideous bunch.

"Open your eyes, Mrs Quick! Can't you see what's happening? *Death*. You and I are going to *drown*. AND ALL YOU GIVE A..."

Dee-Dee folded Glory under her wing as though she were a delicate egg. "Shh, Gloria, it's time you were back in your bed." She glared at Mrs Quick, her disgust clear in the sudden dropped tone of her voice, "Shame on you."

Mrs Quick's roaring hot anger boiled over into icy coldness. She patted her tea-stained dress with the corner of a floury tea-towel and took a long hard look at her diamond-encrusted wristwatch. "Four o'clock," she sighed and added in a steely tone, "you have half an hour to get you and your wood-worm hand to the emporium to make my cane before Master Sharp

arrives at eight. You will not be late. OR ELSE!"
Mrs Quick peeled off the pointy tip of her broken
fingernail and flicked it over the rows of sugared-
lemon butterflies and onto an enormous round cake
– the smallest tier of five that had yet to be decorated.
"It seems I *might*, after all, need to visit my good
friends at the Fitzroy Hotel to discuss the matter of
their careless baker girl."

Dee-Dee forced Glory to sit back down and
stormed across the kitchen. She grabbed a wooden
spoon and scooped out a crescent of cake where
the fingernail fell. "It's a lemon cake, Mrs Quick…"
She held back the tip of the spoon and flicked it,
catapulting its contents across the kitchen. "… so *you*,
of all people, should know that it's *bitter* enough."

Glory, mouth open, stared at the flecks of sponge
that now adorned Mrs Quick's hat.

"Take your stinking nail and get the hell out of my
kitchen."

Dee-Dee didn't leave Glory's side until she'd
pretended to sleep, relaxing her face and slowing
her breathing, all the while hiding her clenched

fist and pounding heart beneath the bedcovers. Hopping out of bed, veins pumping and head spinning, Glory opened the wardrobe and helped Needle out. "Breathe," she reminded him and stood staring at him until his purple complexion faded away.

Glory opened the window, urged Magpie to stay on the windowsill and gently retrieved the green ragdoll from her beak. With her back turned to Needle, she quickly squeezed out the rainwater that soaked its green threads and hugged it. She took a sideways glance at Needle who, with hands on his hips and eyebrows arched, appeared to be awaiting an apology; she had, after all, believed Mrs Quick, if only for a minute.

"I *knew* Mrs Quick was lying, you know," she said as she placed her ragdoll back into her bag along with the shop key and folded list of names, now badly blurred and torn at the edges. She changed the subject, not knowing what colour her words were appearing. "There are too many problems that need fixing, Needle, and I'm not sure how to do it all. How *do* we save lives? *My* life?" She urgently searched the waistband of her dress in search of its button, specially sewn into all her outfits for the sole purpose of hanging her bag.

"You're inside out," offered Needle as he pointed at the seams running through the folds of her dress.

"I *know* that. I can't change it now 'cause it'll bring me bad luck. And if the flood doesn't get me, let there be no doubt Mrs Quick surely will – one way or the other." She plucked a threaded needle from her pincushion and ripped a button from her sleeve's cuff. "And how do we free your poor papa, all banged up like that? No one will listen to *us*." She looked Needle and herself up and down with pity in her eyes. "Believe me, I tried warning them. I told the police and screamed it to the crowd that stood over me when they pulled me from the river. I was blue in the face. I told the doctor – I was shouting it out, over and over, until he went and jabbed me with something that knocked me for six!" she cried as she pulled up her sleeve to show off her bandage. "I told Dee-Dee, too, and no one believed me. And you Needle? Did you warn no one?" pleaded Glory as she sewed the button to her waistband, snapped the thread with great drama and hung her bag.

Needle grabbed his cheeks. "I… I… couldn't…"

He scratched his head and smiled an awkward smile at Glory. It was one thing to stand on his imaginary podium telling treasure tales to his mother or Magpie; it was entirely another to find the right words of doom for a crowd of busy, horn-tooting strangers who always appeared to be late for an important engagement.

"This is no time for letting the cat get your tongue!" said Glory, a harsh dig that brought lip-pulling bakery thugs to Needle's mind. "SPEAK UP, I tell you, and mark my words because, in case you haven't noticed, mine are red, Needle. RED! RED! RED!" cried Glory so loudly she risked another visit from her sister. "Did you *not* even do a *thing* to get your papa out?"

Needle saw red, but this time it was his own. "HOW? HOW DO I BE DOING THAT?"

Glory cupped her hand across his mouth, "Shush!"

He spread out his hands. Like black spots on a bad potato, they were peppered with peeled blisters. "I pulled and pulled at them jail bars when you be sleeping," he muffled through her fingers. "I be throwing rocks at them guards until they throwed rocks back and chased me down roads that ain't even in Inthington – *my* Inthington." He hammered his temple with his fist, "I don't have what it takes to save Da."

"Oh, forgive me, Needle," Glory pleaded as she moved her hand to his fist and held it gently until he dipped his head. When he began to pick at his fingernails inches from the tip of his nose, she continued, "Look, it's probably all the better you didn't show your face out there – the police believe you and your papa came to Inthington with a plan to rob Master Sharp's invention. They say it's too much of a coincidence that you turned up just before his visit and tried to help a thief break out of jail."

"A *THIEF?*"

"Shush! Sorry – I meant *your papa*. I know he's no thief, but they wouldn't listen – they even waved a newspaper under my nose that had his photograph and a big headline – THE SHARP THIEF. And they're saying you're his apprentice. It's all down to *me*," she concluded, "*I* have to tell everyone – tell every passing person I meet even if it kills me. Because if I don't, it *will* kill me, and thirteen others. I have to go." Glory pulled an orange shawl from her wardrobe and tied it around her shoulders. She let out a sarcastic giggle.

"And to think that blasted walking cane was my biggest worry!" If she didn't show up today and make a walking cane worthy of Lord Buckram and his treasured guest – what did it really matter? Of course, she'd be jobless for life, however long that life would last.

As Glory tied the ribbon of her hat, Needle threw his satchel over his shoulder, mumbling something under his breath about needing courage to speak up. Not only was his friend's life at stake, but one of those lost souls she spoke of was his father and there was no way on this earth that he was going home without him. He forced his raw toes against the pebbles in his boot and looked at Glory.

Eye to eye, they made a plan.

It would be dangerous, of course, with him being hunted by the police, but they would high-tail it to the centre of Inthington and warn every passer-by, shopkeeper, street trader and motorcar passenger about the Great Flood. According to the plaque, it would happen on the 6th January and that day was almost done.

Chapter Seventeen

When it was time, Magpie did exactly what Needle asked, and her relentless pecking at the kitchen window soon tore Glory's sister away from her final, bubbling pot of lemon curd. Despite her looming deadline to deliver her five-tiered cake with its butterfly decorations to the gallery by eight o'clock, Magpie had succeeded in distracting her. Dee-Dee stood at the back door, just in from the driving rain, pulling stretches of raw dough to form tiny, delicious balls between her fingers and tossed them, one at a time, at the intriguing crow that danced before her.

"Now!" Needle whispered to Glory having seen from the back bedroom window that Magpie had her sister entertained. They tiptoed down the stairs, closed the front door quietly and, when they reached the end of the terrace, Needle whistled. Magpie dipped her farewell to Dee-Dee and joined Glory and Needle as they wormed their way through tight laneways and back alleys in the lashings of rain, not bothering to jump over the ankle-deep puddles that covered more ground than not.

With Magpie sweeping overhead, they continued along the River Notion, past the glass-fronted haberdashery and glut of fashion boutiques that once housed the bakery and button factories. It was the end of the working day for workers as they stepped out into the deluge, umbrellas clashing while tyres splashed muddy water and horns honked impatiently.

No one noticed them as they ran alongside the embankment wall that butted up to the foreshore and no one appeared to notice something else that was sprinting and rushing and heaving before their very eyes: the river.

With Eyelet Bridge coming into sight, Needle stopped. Trying desperately to catch his breath, he leaned on the low wall and stared with wild eyes into the roaring mass before him.

"It be coming! The flood – LOOK!"

A river-load of melted snow and the relentless rain were leaving their mark on the River Notion. It swelled higher than either had ever seen before and, like a herd of beasts, its usual ripples were replaced with angry, chopping waves. Needle looked down to the foreshore, now entirely drowned beneath the racing black water. His eye followed the rush of tide – still outward bound to the sea – and, in the distance to his left, broken branches reached up out of the water and scratched at the underbelly of Eyelet Bridge's five arches.

Never before had Needle felt so small, so fragile.

He turned and scanned the men and women that blindly bustled along the quay. He'd considered them important and powerful, but suddenly they seemed so weak. The river was wider, faster, *stronger* than them as it raged through the town. Its roar was black – pitch black – a roar that howled and laughed and jeered at the oblivious life around it.

"It'll be bursting its banks and throwing everyone onto their backs," cried Needle, his voice inaudible to even his own ears. He could see the raging river twisting off their boots and pulling at their lips just like those bakery thugs had done to him. Taking their breath away.

"Look, over there!" Needle read on Glory's lips. Opposite them, on the far side of the river, the bulging water climbed high up the jail walls and was feet from the first row of windows.

"HE BE GOING TO DROWN!" roared Needle. Was Da still trapped in his cell watching the water rise? A cell that would soon be under water? Did those jail officers even care? He kicked the wall at his feet and smashed his fists against his temples. Da was just a thief to them! This plan of theirs to have the guts to stand before strangers and have them believe their unbelievable story, was hopeless enough. To expect their warning to reach the ears of all fourteen souls, not to mention convince the officers to move the prisoners to safety, was simply ridiculous.

Exasperated, Needle crumbled to his knees.

Glory grabbed his elbow. "Your papa told no lies when he said you had courage. I've seen it with my own eyes – you *do* have what it takes. A bucket load. We have to start somewhere. We can warn everyone. We can do it."

Needle pulled his wet hair across his forehead and looked into Glory's eyes.

"Cross my heart," she added.

Magpie, at the base of a tree to Glory's side, hammered her feet off the sodden ground: *Trust me*.

As hard as it was, he would try to believe them. He had little choice, in the end; the only two people he had in this strange world were in trouble – one stood before him, bursting with determination, and the other was trapped just a river's width away.

"We can do it," he reassured himself, although it sounded more like a question than a fact.

Glory grabbed his hand and they sped off in the direction of Eyelet Bridge. "I know just the place where everyone will hear us – over there." Glory pointed towards Magpie who had landed on a large stone plinth of several tiers, still under construction, at the nearest corner of Eyelet Bridge. When they arrived at it they ripped away the metal fencing that protected its base and stood before several blocks that led up to a flat, square platform. Glory hitched up her skirt and began to climb. "They're building this for Master Sharp. They've a gigantic statue of the man ready to go – I've seen a picture of it in the Inthington

Times. I think they're just waiting for the weather to pick up so they can stick it down or something." Glory stood at the top, ten feet up at least, hands on hips.

A horn honked in disapproval. The tram driver rolled down his fogged-up window. "Hoodlum! Get down! That's Master Sharp's monument – have you any respect?"

"WE'RE ON AN IMPORTANT MISSION," hollered Glory and she dismissed the man and his disapproving passengers with her fist. "Come on Needle, get up here. Everyone can see us. You too, Magpie!"

Needle cupped his hands before his mouth, breathing the same air over and over again – just as his mother would make him do with old newspaper anytime he was faced with the overwhelming desire to avoid a situation. It was time to speak up. He told himself that all he had to do was repeat whatever Glory was about to say. That way, he didn't have to think of the right words and surely that would make things half as difficult.

He climbed up one block. On the second block, a perfect rectangular indent was prepared and waiting for its plaque. He knew, from the second he laid eyes on it, it was precisely the same size as his jigsaw of shards.

"That be where they'll end up putting it, I reckon – the plaque." He pointed to it and turned his head away, fearing he was seeing an unwanted future. Magpie hopped up and stood still as a statue beside the empty rectangle.

"Get your mouth and your behind up here NOW or I'll be adding your name to those shards, Needle Luckett."

With Needle finally by her side, Glory began. "HEAR YE! HEAR YE! … That's how they do it," she assured Needle. "HEAR YE!" She beckoned passers-by with her wooden hand. They flicked their umbrellas and continued gossiping about Master Sharp's invitation list. "Oi! Are you deaf? Stop walking, you with the fancy hat. WE HAVE IMPORTANT NEWS…"

Glory poked Needle's shoulder, good and sharp.

Needle cleared his throat. "HEAR… Ouch!" A hard scone with burnt berries stung his ear. A second sizable piece soon followed, hitting Glory on her shoulder.

"Oh!" Glory spun on her stage and stopped to face the culprits – she found a group of three boys and a girl, all well-dressed yet umbrella-less. Raising her finger, she opened her mouth, only for a confetti of soggy crumbs to smash into her teeth. The lucky throwers pushed each other around and splashed on the footpath below in celebration.

"What's wrong, little girl? Need a *hand*?" yelled one boy. He was solid, Needle noticed, pure muscle, and he wasn't sure if it was the fashion of the day, but he wore an overcoat too short and too tight for much comfort. His face was square, his neck thick and his arms were very long.

Glory's lips puckered, ready to spew red words, and it served to egg the boy on. "Go on, tell us what else is wooden! Your tongue?" Forcing the rest of his scone into his own mouth, he nudged his friends to take over, tipping a pebble towards the one girl in the gang. She had long blonde hair and a familiar royal-blue, gold-buttoned coat. *Mrs Selvage's daughter from the emporium*. Glory had no doubt a stolen Frippery & Fandangle fine gold chain still sat in her pocket.

"*YOU?* You robbing…"

The not so 'good' girl, who was supposedly in a class ahead of Glory in more ways than one, flung the pebble high, aiming for Glory's legs. Needle made efforts to stand in its path but Glory shoved him clear and, using her shin, kicked it back.

"Ouch!" cried Glory as she hopped precariously on one leg. Needle grabbed her wooden hand to steady her only to have it skim the tip of his nose as though she were swatting a fly. "I *don't* need help," she hissed before pointing to the girl. "Not sure your snob of a mother would be too happy seeing her good little girl doing that."

The boy shoved the girl forward a few steps, urging her to keep at it.

"Come down here and say that to my face," demanded the girl. She looked over her shoulder at the boy, perhaps seeking approval.

Glory put her hands on her hips and stuck out her tongue.

Needle began his descent. He was always told he had two choices in such a situation and he was happy to stick with the one he always tried to choose – *flee*, if he was still standing. He wouldn't have to *give as good as he got* as his father would say if he wasn't around to have 'gotten' anything in the first place.

"We be leaving now, we be leaving now," Needle whispered. As soon as he turned his back, the strong boy grabbed him tight from behind, wrapping his long arms around Needle's stomach, trapping his satchel against his back.

"GET OFF HIM!" roared Glory. She jumped down from several blocks up, causing Needle to flinch. There were no stones around the base of the plinth, so Glory urgently reefed her bag out from her skirt and ripped its tassels to pull out anything to throw in revenge – she found the heavy key to the emporium.

Rosie Selvage stood before Glory. "*Now* you can say it to my face." As thin as she was, she towered over Glory. Her face was bright red from all she was feeling and it was spreading fast in great blotches down her long neck.

"I'll show your face…" Glory raised up her hand, ready to defend herself with a very dangerous key.

"Don't do it!" Needle yelled, pulling at the arms and kicking the legs of his sweaty captor.

"Look at my shin," shouted Glory, hooking her skirt and revealing a pebble-made trail of blood.

"Throwing that key be locking more doors than you know," warned Needle. He raised his hand as high as the boy's hold would allow and pointed towards the distant jail. "Besides, I don't be knowin' about this fella…" He flicked his head back, nearly butting the boy who gripped him tight, "but you might hurt the one bit of good in that one." He nodded towards the girl between them.

The blonde girl's stiff shoulders appeared to drop several inches.

Glory sent a look his way that made him gulp. "I didn't hear her red, Glory – only orange," he added in his defence.

The girl backed up a step, bumping into Needle's shoulder. She gave him a look – *shame*, perhaps? – and Needle wondered if it was the first time someone had bothered to tell her she wasn't entirely bad.

"ROSIE!" The boy spat.

"Shut it, Marcus, you oaf," said the girl.

Glory cocked her head and opened her eyes a little wider – she had not expected that.

"There's little hope for my brother," Rosie said to Needle. She edged closer, close enough for Needle to stop fidgeting and push back against the boy. "See, there's not one bit of good in *him*. Not even a scrap," she warned, "but *I'm* sorry." She firmly instructed her brother to snap out of it and turned to Glory,

"Sorry to you, too." She walked off, her long, blonde hair confidently swishing side to side across her shoulders.

"See? *One bit of good*, I reckon," reported Needle, glad that he'd listened to his mother when she'd debated with his father that advising their son to hit back was not the best thing to do; if you knocked out the last bit of someone's good with a right-hook, she warned, they could end up being good-less for ever.

Marcus tightened his grip. Needle was struggling to breathe.

"Let him go," Glory pleaded.

"Not until we've been paid for our services," Marcus spat into Needle's ear. Two spindly boys either side of him slipped their fingers into Needle's coat pockets. One pulled out a handful of sixty-four-year-old fluff, the other a shiny, 1920s edition silver pocket-knife.

"Nice," hissed the taller of the two. He studied the pocket-knife up close and licked its metal handle. He snapped it open.

"PAPA'S KNIFE!" cried Glory.

"GIVE IT BACK!" roared Needle. For once, his words came easily – he knew what that knife meant to her; that knife had the power to bring back her father, if only in her mind. He twisted his body, trying desperately to free his arms.

Glory lunged forward. "YOU STOLE MY PAPA'S KNIFE!"

Lightning fast, the boy held the knife high, well out of reach, only to drop his arm again. He was *not* her target.

"How could you? How could you? How *could* you?" Glory cried. She beat her fist on Needle's shoulder. "How could you do that to me? My papa's knife?"

Realising her words, her blue, blue words, were aimed at him and not at the spindly pickpocket to his side, Needle tried hard to say something. "I…"

"YOU'RE A THIEF."

"But I never stole noth—"

"A LYING thief," she screamed into his face.

He stared back into her eyes.

Shocked, Glory accepted the stare but she knew something had changed; that moment felt broken and icy cold. Their special connection, and any trust and friendship that came with it, was suddenly carved to pieces.

With Mrs Quick's sneers and her sister's 'told-you-so' in her ears, Glory ran and ran, far away from her knife-thieving, back-stabbing, so-called friend. As daylight faded and rain blackened the evening skies, she passed the clocktower and turned onto Crossgrain Street, stopping at the junction of two busy roads. She leaned against the curved window of Inthington's oldest apothecary, using its grey and black striped awning for shelter. The traffic lights before her turned red and, as though she were being pulled by an invisible thread, all motorcars seemed to stop and stare, urging her to cross.

She had arrived at the front entrance of the Frippery & Fandangle Emporium – a place she would be unlikely to step foot in again. Parting her dripping wet hair, she looked through blurry eyes at its large windows, bedecked with glittering jewels and sparkling lights. She promised herself something with a big cross of her heart: from now on, she would never, ever be so impetuous, so reckless, so trusting, and so utterly impatient that she didn't give herself the time to simply stop and think.

Chapter Eighteen

"GO AWAY!"

Glory hid Needle's face with her wooden hand so she wouldn't be swayed by his eyes and, instead, focussed her own on Frippery & Fandangle's window display. She pretended to admire a bracelet that she had created only one week earlier as it sparkled in the last of the daylight.

Needle took a step back on hearing her red words and pulled her father's pocket-knife from his pocket.

"But I got it back! Look! I swapped it for Da's old bone comb and a marble." Needle stuck out his chest. He'd been proper brave, standing up to that Marcus boy, and surely once Da found out, he'd be proud – so proud that maybe he wouldn't mind losing two of his favourite things. Wouldn't he be glad they didn't want his bottle of green medicine, not to mention the drawer handle? Just the comb and marble. "I put them in my silver beetle box and gave them the lot – I be thinking it was the box that did it."

Glory snatched the pocket-knife from Needle's hand and pushed it up her sleeve. "Keep your thieving paws away from me," she spat and turned her back to him.

"Ah, Glory, you got to believe me – I didn't steal nothin' from you. Or the shop. There be a big difference between robbing and—"

Glory poked him between his eyes. "LIAR!" More tears appeared out of goodness knows where and she slapped her own eyes in frustration. Now that he had lied about stealing her pocket-knife, her mind spiralled, beginning to doubt it all. "Was *every* word out of your mouth a lie? The flood? Was *that* a lie? You made me think I was going to *die*! And your stupid treasure stories? All that nonsense about the hot shards and the past, and your papa… and… and… the bird?" she squealed as Magpie arrived at her feet. Glory scooped her up. She was bedraggled, with feathers poking out at odd angles making her eyes appear owl-like and sad. "Oh! Not you too, Magpie?"

she howled into her ruffled feathers. All her red talk faded back to blue. "Needle, how *could* you?"

"I am *not* a *liar*!" said Needle with almost complete confidence (he spared a quick thought for the coin's story of the rich jeweller lady when they were under the bridge and reasoned that the story *could* be true, just not yet). "Not one bit of it is a lie," he cried, quickly crossing his heart on both sides with both hands, over and over again.

"*Prove* it," demanded Glory.

"HOW?" Needle pounded at his temples and spun on the spot. How could he prove his word was good, always? "Lying hurts. *Really* hurts me. In here," he said

as he pointed to his chest. "And here. And here." He added his mind and his stomach to his list. "I didn't steal nothing – I *borrowed* your da's knife, I *borrowed* Mrs Quick's things and people *are* going to drown and I CAN'T BE FIXING THAT ON ME OWN. They'll all die! *My da* will die, *you* will…" He rubbed his nose on his sleeve. "Just stop for once and think about it, Glory."

"*Stop and think?* That's exactly what I've done, you fool!" said Glory. She bit her lip and stepped into the emporium's porch out of the relentless rain. Perhaps she needed to 'stop' a bit more? Within seconds of seeing the pocket-knife being plucked from Needle's pocket, she ran and ran. And that was hardly stopping and thinking, now was it?

With a huff, she said, "If you were telling the truth, you *would* be able to prove it, wouldn't you?" She wondered if he'd see the last bit of hope in her words, whatever their colour might be.

The 'Shop Closed' sign smacked the inside of the door's glass.

Glory froze.

Needle pulled his ears out to the side.

"Yes, Officer Pocket. Right now, outside my shop.

222

Both of them, I dare say. They've returned to finish what they—"

Needle barged past Glory and boldly pushed open the door. "Mrs Quick? Put down your candlestick."

Like a cornered dog, Mrs Quick bared her teeth and growled. She held her telephone to her chest, tangling its curling wires in her countless necklaces.

"Every bit of your cane be ready and waiting. Isn't that right, Glory?"

"Needle!" cried Glory. He was standing next to Mrs Quick, chest out with his hand behind his back, schoolmaster style. "Mrs Quick, I'm not sure but maybe he *is* a thie—"

"I BE *LIKE* A THIEF!" interrupted Needle, as loud as his nerves would allow, and pointed at his ragged clothes. "I *look* like one so I can be listening to their plans, those crooks you been gossiping about. Every bit of your cane is safely hidden, Mrs Quick. Can't be saying where though." He glanced through the open door at the steady flow of umbrella-laden passers-by. "Too many ears around here, if you catch my drift." He stood closer to Mrs Quick and tipped the side of his nose. He turned to Glory and mouthed, "*I can prove it.*"

Glory shut her wide open mouth.

Mrs Quick dropped her earpiece, pulled a silk handkerchief from her sleeve and covered her mouth, only releasing it slightly to shout at Glory. "Where is it? Where is the cane? Bring it to me NOW!"

"Just one small matter of the, eh, candlestick," said Needle.

"Ahem. He means *telephone*."

With an angry snap, Mrs Quick detangled the telephone, sending a shower of loose pearls racing across the floor like cold water bubbles on a hot pan. She changed her tone to that normally reserved for filthy rich shoppers. "Officer Pocket, my dear friend…" She turned her back and muttered something about it being a long day and the 'thieves' were, in fact, her customers having been caught in the torrential rain. Returning the telephone to the counter, she turned to Glory and hissed, "Bring it to the gallery, eight o'clock. Or it's the gutters."

Needle calmly walked out of the emporium, grabbing a stunned Glory by the sleeve as he passed.

Glory tried to pull him to a stop as he marched, taller than before, past the clocktower and on towards the river. "A hidden cane? Did you just tell another lie?" she asked, unsure if that was what he'd actually done. "Is lying *that* easy for you? Did fibbing hurt? There?" She attempted to poke him in the stomach as she tried to keep up. "Where else did you say it hurts? There?" She slapped his wet hair. "NEEDLE! Are you a liar or are you not? You said you could prove it!"

When they reached the quay, Needle stopped outside a well-lit ribbon shop and, with Glory on his tail, climbed up several steps to its door. He pointed towards Eyelet Bridge, its view partially obscured by a small crowd as they stared in awe at the power of the River Notion. Magpie squawked from above and landed on his outstretched arm.

"If I be lying about the flood – there be your proof. LOOK at it! LOOK!" He gently poked Glory's cheek so that she stopped studying his eyes and faced the murderous, raging force that was thundering through the town. "And if I be lying about the hot shards..." he cried as he grappled with his satchel. He punched his fist into the shirt cotton that held the shards and yelled as his knuckles met their heat. Magpie pecked at the slush, willing Needle to take some for his hand. He layered some of it onto his fist and lowered his voice, "I didn't want to be proving it this way but if I be lying about me reading treasures, how would I know your da gave you that pocket-knife the morning he died with a tiny bird he'd only half carved? I knows that because I felt the knife's story."

"Papa's robin?" Glory cupped her hand over her mouth and ignored the tears that began to fall. Magpie hopped up onto Glory's boot and leaned against her leg. "You *were* telling the truth about reading treasures?"

"Yeah. And I be sorry," whispered Needle. Not sure what to do, he awkwardly reached across to Glory and stopped one big teardrop with his finger. He watched as the determined tear split into two as it spilled over his nail and flowed down her cheek in two thin lines. He took a deep breath. "And your cane? Well, I told no lie there too. I told your Mrs Quick it be all waiting and you can see for yourself if you give me a chance to show you. I did *not* lie and I *can* prove it." He shook the slush from his knuckles and showed her his hand. "But it be up to you if you want to believe it."

"Blisters!" cried Glory as she held his hand in hers, turning it towards the light from the ribbon shop window. "The shards *are* hot. You were telling no lies about that either, were you?"

"No lies."

"And you were borrowing Papa's pocket-knife?" she asked but quickly put her hand to his lips. "No need to answer—"

A distant shriek grabbed their attention as an untethered boat crashed its way through the first gap of Eyelet Bridge.

"Time be running out," Needle warned. Ignoring the force of the pebbles hidden deep in the toes of his boots, he took off at some speed towards the bridge.

Glory watched him go.

She stopped to think. Not once had he stuttered. Not once had he faltered or struggled to find the right words. Had it all come straight from his soul, skipping the muddle and worry of his mind? The raging river, the half-carved robin, the blistered knuckles...

She pushed up her soggy sleeves, forced her pocket-knife into the mouth of her bag and sprinted. "WAIT FOR ME!" she called after him, soon reaching his side. "We need to get warning. We could try the plinth again? Or down by the markets? Or the…" She came to a sudden stop, standing ankle-deep in an oily puddle. "Sure what's the blasted point?"

Needle stopped and turned to face her. He said nothing but asked with his eyebrows.

"It's just… Agh! *No one* will listen to me!" She held up her wooden hand and shook it as though she wanted it to drop to the ground between them. "They won't listen to you either! That's the thing about this town – it's all about who you are. You have to *be* a voice, before you get heard."

Needle scratched his head.

"*What?* Spit it out," ordered Glory on seeing his confused expression.

He squinted in the rain, now being whipped and swirled by the growing wind. "How… how do you *be* a voice?"

"What I mean is you need to be rich or famous, someone who's special, held in the highest regard."

"Like your Master Sharp?"

Glory's eyes opened wide with delight. She raced up to Needle and hugged him tight. She pulled away and, despite his bruises, poked him hard on the forehead. "See, Needle Luckett? Sometimes if you actually open your mouth and say something, you get it so, so right!"

"Huh?"

"*Master Sharp* – when he speaks, all the great people of Inthington, not to mention the rest, will listen!" she shouted over the five chimes that boomed from the clocktower. She pounded onwards along the river, holding herself at a peculiar angle as though crossing the finish line in a sprint. "All we need to do is warn Master Sharp and *he'll* warn everyone. He'll be arriving in the Millbank Gallery at eight o'clock... so if we get into the building and... Agh!" Her plan fell flat along with her new found energy. She smacked herself on the forehead with the butt of her palm. "If only we had the stupid cane to deliver – without an invitation that's the only way we'd ever get in."

Needle smiled, hooked her arm and ran.

Chapter Nineteen

As Needle helped her into his trove, Glory was shivering uncontrollably from the fear of falling from Eyelet Bridge's slippery blocks. Once inside, where the violent sound of the river was dampened by the thick stone of the bridge, she was surrounded by an impenetrable darkness. She couldn't even see her own hands.

Needle whistled a yellow tune. Her breathing calmed.

Blindly rummaging in his satchel, Needle found the silver tin that he'd rescued from his father's bag – it was not unlike his own beetle tin and kept his father's supply of matches dry. He lit a candle and she could see.

The flame from the very old stub of candle danced

merrily on a corner shelf just above the sad remains of a nest. Magpie pecked at its rotted surface and rocked from side to side in an effort to settle in.

Needle kicked a layer of dust with his boots. "Da and me call this place our trove. This is where he showed me how to make things with them treasures I dig up and he teached me how to listen to their stories right here, in this very spot." Needle gently turned Glory's shoulders in the direction of his driftwood workbench, now pitched at an angle and supported on one side with borrowed orange bricks – until last night they had blocked the entrance to his trove.

He pointed to the workbench. "For you, Glory."

Glory gasped. Her eyes filled with tears.

She pointed at her face and confirmed with a gentle squeal, "Happy tears!" She wiped them away with her soggy orange shawl and hugged Needle so tightly that rainwater dripped from his coat and onto the floor. He looked down at their pock-marks dotting the inch-thick dust and felt himself blush.

Magpie squawked and spread her wings wide.

"Oh, Needle! I guess Magpie couldn't bring me a cane, so she brought me you instead. You did all this? For me?"

She didn't wait for his reply, grabbed the stool and sat. Hanging before her, by way of antique brass tacks on a strip of wood, were all her fine sketches of the walking cane that, only yesterday, hung in the emporium. Grubby fingerprints told a tale that Needle had studied them for more than just a short while. Overnight, Needle had fished everything from the wall of mahogany drawers back at the Emporium, and, where the drawers failed to deliver, he had scratched and dug at the diminishing foreshore by moonlight until he found treasure worthy of her designs.

"And there be your tools," said Needle as he pointed to a row of instruments. Glory blindly pulled her father's pocket-knife from her bag and laid it alongside.

"I was glad you was sleeping all night, safe and all, but I be thinking you were sleeping away your job too. I borrowed it all but couldn't make it," he admitted as he sighed at the exquisite drawings. "Only you can do that."

Glory shook her head at how foolish she'd been. On sight of a torn piece of bootlace from Mrs Quick's purse and then her father's knife hidden in Needle's pocket, she had not once, but twice jumped to the wrong conclusion.

"This cane be our last chance – like you said, the only way we be getting into the gallery to warn Master Sharp is if we be having something important to deliver." He twisted the dial on his father's old pocket-watch and listened carefully for ticks. "It be just after five, right? Gives you three hours to make it, Glory." He placed it, face up, beside the tools.

Glory turned, looked at Needle and held up her wooden hand. "But… THIS!"

"You can do it, Glory," offered Needle, kindly.

Biting her lip, Glory made some effort to calm her growing frustration but, like a shook bottle of fizzy lemon, it soon overflowed. "You think I can 'do it', do you? REALLY?" Glory hissed as she picked up her tweezers and snapped them shut like angry jaws. "Have you ever tried to fasten a gem-claw? Have you? Or plait a wire of gold, or split a bead, WITH A MISSING HAND? I can do nothing with this lump of wood. When I put the pieces in their place, have a good look because, as soon as you touch it, it'll fall apart." She fired down the tweezers, hid her face in

233

the crook of her elbow and thumped the workbench with her wooden fist.

Needle ran his fingers through his hair. The words forming in his head were beginning to glow red, but he could do little to stop them. "This cane be our last chance, Glory! OUR LAST CHANCE TO SAVE MY DA'S LIFE, for crying out loud. You'll be missing more than a hand if we don't have the cane – YOUR LIFE, GLORY!" He stood still, hands on hips, panting.

Staring blankly at her wooden hand, Glory's bottom lip wobbled.

Needle shook his head. "I be sorry about that, Glory, them words wouldn't stop coming out." He tested the strength of a wooden box with two hands before turning it on its side beside Glory's stool. He sat on it and inched as close to her as he could. "You be right – you *do* be missing something," he said as he struggled with the string tucked under his collar. "But it's not your hand. I seen you tie your bag with two fingers. I seen you plait your messy hair," he added and pointed to her head, choosing to ignore the shocked look on her face. "You tie bootlaces like they be fun and you climbed a wet wall with moss to cling on to. You sewed foxes on your curtain, so small I had to squint. The only thing stopping you from making something that does *not* fall apart is your rushing. There be a word for people like you."

"A word?" huffed Glory. "Go on then, spit it out! You think I'm what? *Impatient?*"

Needle wasn't sure if he should agree; it was a long word and he had a good idea what it meant but, by the way she said it, it sounded mean and that was not his intention.

"To hell with patience!" Glory continued, "or is *impulsive* the word for me? Or why not go the whole hog and just call me *impetuous* like Mrs—"

"Stop!" said Needle. He wasn't sure what any of the words meant but instinct, not to mention their angry colour, told him she wasn't so pleased. He shook his head and chose his words carefully, afraid blue smoke might appear from her ears. "All I be knowing is you need to slow down your thinking." He pulled his necklace's stone with its perfect hole through his collar and held it up between them.

"What's that?" Though her nostrils still flared with every breath, her anger quickly made way for curiosity.

"It be a hag stone. And it can give you exactly

what you be missing – your patience, or whatever you call it. I can tell you it took patience for the river to flow at this stone until it made that perfect hole." He stuck the tip of his little finger through it. "Just like your walking cane, it takes patience for things to be born."

Glory took the stone from Needle's grip, taking care not to pull its string too tight around his neck, and rubbed her finger across its silky surface.

"Story has it, if you look through the hole, you can see a whole other world – a better world. A world where things can be just the way you want them to be." He leaned closer and urged her to look through its hole.

"What am I looking for?" Glory whispered as she squinted and held it right up to her lashes.

"Patience."

As she peered through the hole, the world she saw through it may not have appeared different, but a gentle smile slowly spread across her face. He heard her sigh out all her frustration along with her impatience.

"Now imagine your cane – just the way you want it."

Glory held her breath while she did. "Thanks, Needle," she said, warmly, "but I've only three hours…"

"I know, and I'll help." Needle tucked the hag stone back under his collar and placed his right hand on the workbench before her. "You can use my *left* hand," he said with a cheeky grin and a wink. "This *is* my right, yeah?" he quickly checked. "Now tell me what it needs to be doing first."

Glory smiled at Needle's squinted eyes, full of concentration. This Needle beside her was brave and bursting with pride but, when she looked down at his hand, she noticed its slight tremble. So, just like Needle would whisper to his hands and feet as he scaled his walls, Glory told his hand not to worry and began her instructions to hold a gem here or twist something there.

Each piece was held firmly by Needle as Glory tweaked them all until they sang to her and, soon, using the line of ingredients before her, she added the last few gems; happy ovals of yellow amber. As Needle twisted the cane's ball-shaped handle, it sparkled in the candlelight. It was a perfect copy of Glory's sketches, right down to the unfinished, blank bit on her drawing: the final piece that would sit proudly at the top of the cane's handle. It was yet to be considered and it needed to be something special.

Glory frowned as her eyes desperately searched the workbench for a piece that would work.

"If you don't mind, Glory. I thought maybe this would do…" Using his rusted tweezers, he fished out the triangular metal shard from his satchel – the first piece he had pulled from the mud – and held it up high.

Glory tilted her head and read its words.

"*In Memory of,*" she read on the first line, "And below that it says *the Great*. That's perfect, Needle… *In Memory of the Great!*"

Needle beamed. "You take it – it only be hot for me." He placed the shard in Glory's hand, "And Da, of course." The mention of his father's name made his heart race. He pictured him stuck, or worse, drowning, in the depths of the jail.

Glory noticed his anxious glance at the pocket-watch. She picked up her sharp pointed tool that trembled on the workbench in time with Needle's hopping leg. "Let's get this done." She softened the shard's hard edges, polished it until it shone bright as a mirror, and placed it on the top of the handle. Aqua opals were placed all around it until they met with the diamonds and amber stones already in place. Finally, the completed handle was placed on a polished stick of oak and finished with a foot of solid silver.

It was *spectacular,* just as Lord Buckram demanded, not to mention *exceptional, outstanding* and *astonishing quality.* In fact, Needle thought, it was more than that: it was *important* – so important, it was going to get them to Master Sharp and it was going to save his father's life and Glory's life and the lives of all the fine people of Inthington.

Chapter Twenty

With the cane now wrapped in his coat and tucked into his belt, Needle nudged it higher up his back. He surveyed the crowd that swarmed the gallery's entrance. Men and women shuffled their way up twenty wide steps, all hunched under umbrellas and pulling ugly faces at the rain. They were dressed like shiny coins – not bent ones that hid in the mud, but new ones Mam would bring home from her market stall. Needle gulped and tucked in his shirt.

Glory poked him. "Keep moving! That's Lord Buckram up there." She pointed at a man who stood poker-straight welcoming guests inside the arched entrance. Dragging Needle by the arm, she zig-zagged her way up, taking two steps at a time.

With only four steps left to go, a hand grabbed Glory's hair and yanked it hard.

"AAGH! GET OFF!"

Needle grabbed Mrs Quick's arm but she threatened him with her umbrella. With a firm grip on Glory's hair, she forced them away from the gallery's entrance and trapped them between a large side-window and a statue of a horned beast under attack.

"GIVE IT TO ME!"

Glory cried in pain as Mrs Quick pulled her hair hard. "Take your hands off me, you wicked—"

"HA! You're a cornered animal. And what did you think? That Buckram would dare let you step inside his gallery? LOOK AT YOU! You belong in a freak show…" Mrs Quick shook Glory's ripped hairs from her bony hand and bucked her face right up against Glory's. "Now give me my cane, or else…" She grabbed Glory's fingers on her left hand and bent them backwards. A black silk butterfly pinged off her headband and stuck to Glory's cheek.

Glory fell backwards. Her head hit the glass of the window with a whack.

A muffled cry from inside the foyer hit Needle's ears and he turned to see Lord Buckram glaring through the window, with hands held wide to hold back his guests. He took a step towards them.

"LET GO!" roared Glory as Mrs Quick wrapped her arm around hers to leverage a stronger, breakable grip on her fingers.

"Take it! Just take it!" cried Needle. He flung the cane, still wrapped in his coat, against Mrs Quick. "Glory's made what you asked, missus. Now leave her be." Needle stood back. Surely a deal was a deal.

"HA!" Mrs Quick released Glory's fingers, giving them an awkward twist before doing so, and stared into Needle's red face. "Bring your freak back to your gutter, you beggar. She'll never do a day's work in this town again." Mrs Quick stumbled, straightened herself and her headband, and made her way towards the front door. "THIEF!" she yelled to the crowd and pointed back towards Needle.

Needle grabbed Glory's sore hand and, at some speed, they cleared a low stone railing, dropping down to a patch of lawn at ground level. They turned right onto Ribbon Lane, where Mrs Quick's cries were muffled by honking horns and lashing rain. They ducked behind the thick trunk of a leafless chestnut tree.

"We can't give up now," wept Glory as she peeled Mrs Quick's silk butterfly from her face. "A black butterfly? It's a sign of death – DEATH!" She made attempts to whip it off her finger.

Needle looked down Ribbon Lane. Fitzroy Hotel vans clogged up the road and domed, silver trays of hot food – prepared in the hotel's kitchens – were being unloaded. Along the sidewall of the gallery, several arched basement windows, no taller than his shoulder, reached right down to the footpath where a man stood before each.

"Uh-oh. *Police?*"

"Where?" Glory stood out from the trunk. She jumped up and saw countless men in porter caps before her eye fell on the row of diligent guards. "They're protecting Master Sharp's invention." She shook her head and turned her attention back to the front entrance.

"But there be a side door," said Needle, having recalled it from the previous day when they thought they could knock on some doors and save the world.

Glory nodded. As casually as their nerves would allow, they walked down the road and passed the police officers. As they approached the side entrance,

Needle jolted when he heard a red police siren . He looked back towards Broidery Quay where he saw a police motorcar blocking traffic. Mrs Quick was leaning in its window and, holding the coat-wrapped cane like a weapon, she pointed down Ribbon Lane.

"RUN!" cried Needle. With the side entrance crowded, they sped past it and, both looking behind, smashed straight into a smartly dressed waitress.

"GLORIA? Oh, Gloria!" cried Dee-Dee. She held Glory in a tight hug. "Where have you been? Are you hurt?" She patted down Glory's hair and looked her up and down, searching for visible damage. When Glory shook her head, Dee-Dee held Glory's cheeks in her hands. "I went upstairs to find you. To tell you, I *know*… everything you said – the boy, the plaque, the flood… I know it's all true."

"Dee-Dee?"

"There was a bird, a crow. It was tapping on the kitchen window and, when I went out to say hello, it gave me…" She reached into her pocket.

"But NO ONE believes us, Dee-Dee!" cried Glory. "We need to tell Master Sharp, NOW! If *he* says there's a flood, everyone will believe it."

Dee-Dee looked at Needle. "How much time do we have?"

With his feet itching to run, he shrugged and considered his usual *dunno*. But he *did* know; he knew how many inches the river had risen since they climbed out of his trove with Master Sharp's cane on his back. His answer was calculated. "An hour, tops."

"Master Sharp will be impossible to get to…" warned Dee-Dee. "Ah! Unless there is some kind of distraction…" They heard a police whistle and saw torchlight swing in their direction. Dee-Dee spoke quickly, "Get yourselves some uniforms – check every van before they lock them up for the night. HURRY! And find me by the cake." Dee-Dee grabbed Glory's hand and placed something in it.

Glory didn't need to open her fingers. She knew what was in it for she'd seen it before: a square-shaped shard with a circular 1928 date stamp and grooves that announced that she, Gloria Bobbin, aged twelve, of Knittle Lane, was a lost soul.

Dee-Dee walked away, almost definitely accidentally blocking the path of the determined police officer.

"It's the shard," confirmed Glory as they ran in search of uniforms. "Dee-Dee gave me the square shard."

Before they disappeared into the back of the first van, Needle looked up until he spotted Magpie nestled on the sill of one of the gallery's arched windows.

"Fine work, Magpie," he mouthed to his shard-robbing friend, "fine work."

Chapter Twenty-one

Needle stared at his reflection in the mirror that welcomed them just inside the gallery's side entrance.

"OH! CRIKEY!" He felt like a right genius, dressed in his fancy uniform and framed in so much brass like that. He turned his head slightly to one side and checked out his reflection from that angle, too.

Glory kicked his heel. "What the heck is *wrong* with you? Move it." She smacked his fiddling hand away from his bow-tie she'd tied so perfectly and nudged him along several dark corridors. When the lights shone brighter and the noise level rose, she pulled him to a stop. They peeked around a corner. Like a line of busy ants, waiters and waitresses were marching out one set of double-doors and disappearing through another into what appeared to be a steaming kitchen.

Glory pointed to a sign over the first set of doors.

"*Hall of Great Masters*," she whispered. "This is it, Needle. Remember, they think you're the Sharp Thief's apprentice, so keep your head down and try to *blend in*." She adjusted the yellow ribbon in her hair to match everyone else, but tutted on sight of her wooden hand. Her eye followed a waiter whose tray was piled high with crisp, white napkins. Quicker than a mouse, she nipped in, swiped one, and nipped out. She folded it neatly over her wooden hand and pulled Needle close.

"We need to find Dee-Dee, so look out for her cake – it's lemon, Master Sharp's favourite. We can't miss it; it's huge and it's yellow. Grab a tray or something," she added. "Most of theirs are empty so it looks like they've served the main course already." In the strangest example of blending in, she boldly stepped out and interrupted the flow of staff. The sound of clashing trays echoed along the line.

"Glory!" hissed Needle. What on earth was she at? He pushed his body further against the wall.

"Thank you," Glory said to one surprised waitress

and held out her hand. Her voice was the gunmetal-grey of authority and she was being sixteen again. "THANK YOU," she repeated, this time louder but with orange around the edges, and stood there until the girl handed over her tray. The next waiter in line didn't have to be asked. "I'm needed by the cake," she told him. "Where is it?" The waiter shrugged and pointed to the double-doors. "As you were," she said, and marched confidently back to Needle.

"*What?* Close your mouth or you'll be catching flies. It's a trick I learnt from bat face, *Mrs Quick*," she explained. "She's a fake and gets away with it. So I can fake it, too, can't I? Now hold it higher, like this."

A shrill voice bounced along the corridor. "WHO? WHERE IS SHE?" A waitress, dressed like Glory and countless others but with a face clearly stamped with authority, had the tray-less waiter by his arm.

"Oops!" Glory ducked behind Needle and poked him in the ribs with her tray until he had no choice but to trundle through the double-doors.

They entered the Hall of Great Masters.

"WHOA!" Needle's ears popped and his tray wobbled as he instinctively wanted to cover them with his hands.

The noise! The *heat*! The colours! The smells!

It was all far too much.

He froze on the spot.

He didn't know what to expect when Glory spoke of a ball, but the room was ginormous – at least half the length of a football pitch. Everything was shiny, with round tables sitting under no less than ten chandeliers, each as big as an Eyelet Bridge arch. Wet paint still glistened on the walls – a masterpiece of mountains and rivers so real they widened the space by a mile. In the middle of it all, guests clanged knives and forks down onto empty plates and yelled over one another.

"This way," said Glory. She disappeared somewhere to his left.

Needle whispered to his pebble-crushed toes to move on, *keep going* – even his body knew he should not be there, in the ballroom of a grand gallery. The shiniest of things were displayed for all the world to see, unlike his world where treasures kept themselves hidden beneath mud, only to reveal themselves one tantalising bit at a time.

"Oi!" Glory's hooked finger stuck out from its napkin and snagged the frilly bits on his shirt. She was yelling – something about the cake – as she dragged Needle behind her. Skilfully tilting her tray to hide their faces as they passed Mrs Quick's table, she scuttled along the side of the room, pausing beneath each arched window to search for Dee-Dee and her cake.

They came to a sudden stop in front of a small, ruby red curtain that appeared to hide an alcove. Glory backed up a bit, into its folds.

"Shoot! That's Officer Pocket," she said, jerking her hand towards the top corner of the room. A tall officer, all shoulders and no neck, stood behind a long table next to an enormous yellow curtain. "Where the heck is Dee-Dee?" She looked at Needle as though it were his fault.

"I dunno!" He shrugged. But he was *good* at finding things, wasn't he? He rose on his toes, squinted and began to scan the crowd in ever increasing circles – just like he would do in the pebbles and mud back home. He'd hardly started when Glory whacked him with her tray. She urgently nodded towards the top table. Needle shuffled to his left until, through a small gap between flicking headbands and hats, he could see that Lord Buckram had risen from his chair.

DING! DING! DING! The gallery owner carelessly banged his silver spoon against the side of his glass and it appeared to pour a silence over the room.

Every headband feather stood still.

All eyes were on an elderly man who stood to Lord Buckram's side.

"GOOD EVENING!" boomed Master Sharp.

Needle's eyes opened wide. How could two simple words feel so alive? So colourful! He couldn't quite figure out their colour – gunmetal-greys and happy yellows, yet warm honey all at once, just like pebbles on the shore.

Master Sharp walked along the far side of the top table and came out from behind it. His smile spread from person to person as he moved amongst his audience, and chairs shuffled and people ducked for he spoke not only with his words, but with his arms. Suddenly, the crowd erupted into cheers and applause.

Needle tucked his tray between his knees and covered his ears with his hands. He elbowed Glory. "What he be talkin' about?"

"Important things, so shush! Oh! He's coming this way!"

Closer now, Needle took a good look. The man's suit was sharp and his shoes shiny, but his grey hair was in need of a good cut. He kept a short pencil behind his ear, too; one end sharpened to a point, the other chewed to within an inch of its life. Something about that made Needle smile.

With every step Master Sharp took, excitement rose, and so too did his voice. "…AND NOW, I BRING YOU MY LATEST INVENTION…" He spun briskly on his heel, probably aiming to stop when facing the yellow curtain where Lord Buckram stood ready to pull it wide. But he stalled mid-turn.

Master Sharp stared at Needle.

Needle gulped.

The man opened his mouth, but said nothing. His arms dropped to his sides.

There was a whoosh as everyone turned to stare at Needle, too.

Glory automatically swung her napkin-covered hand behind her back. "Uh-oh."

"*What?* I done nothing!" Needle quickly looked himself up and down. Was it his tray, wedged between his knees? His rope belt holding up his smart trousers? Or Da's boots? Did they really give him away? He shuffled where he stood and hid one boot behind the other. "But, sir, please! I... I..." He found himself staring at his fingernails so he picked at them.

"GEEZ, NEEDLE!" Glory leapt into the space between them and swung her wooden hand out before her. "Master Sharp! We need..." Her white napkin slipped from her hand and floated down to the floor.

Mrs Quick jumped up, knocking her chair over, and croaked something.

Then, *silence*. Had the world stopped?

As though electricity was restored, Master Sharp spun around and raised his hands. "Ladies and Gentlemen, it has just come to my attention that there is a slight delay with the arrival of a key part of my demonstration. Isn't it amazing how things come to a standstill when there's a *little* drop of drizzle?" He laughed and was soon joined by the entire room. "It shouldn't take too long," he said as he marched towards the top table, "besides, you know what I always say: where there's a problem, there's..."

"...ALWAYS A SOLUTION!" roared the well versed crowd.

"And the solution is *CAKE*!" He rubbed his hands together. "Ladies and Gentlemen, SHALL WE HAVE CAKE?"

The audience rose from their chairs and clapped, and before Needle could make sense of it all, he was staring up at the face of Lord Buckram.

"Wheel the cake front and centre, young man. Be careful with it. Serve Master Sharp first, of course, and make it a large one. But don't cut it yet – I need to fetch the Master Chef to accompany you."

"C…cake?"

Needle ducked as Lord Buckram swung his arm over Needle's head. With a tut, he pulled the ruby curtain to one side. "*That* cake. And clean your shoes, for goodness' sake." He clicked his heels and turned to Glory. "Miss. You are coming with me." He held her arm in a tight grip and snapped his fingers at Officer Pocket.

"GLORY!" Needle lunged forward, ready to pull her from Lord Buckram's grip.

"Hey!" came a voice from behind, "Don't you know she's well able to save herself?"

Needle spun around. Who said that? "WHOA!" he cried – the cake was spectacular.

Chapter Twenty-two

For one long minute Needle's ears had to endure the cheers of the crowd as he nudged and nudged the enormous cake across the parquet floor. It weighed a tonne. As the table's wheels clunked across each small slat of polished wood, thousands of sugar-coated lemon butterflies – draped down one side of five ginormous tiers – flickered like the crown jewels under the chandeliers' glare. Even after it reached its destination – centre stage, in front of Master Sharp's table – each tier's thick layer of glossy lemon curd wobbled and wobbled.

And so too did his knees.

Needle wiped his face in his hands. It was up to him now, wasn't it? Glory was gone. He glanced at Master Sharp. He was almost within arm's reach yet a queue of eager men and women had lined up, blocking the man's way back to his seat. Each flapped papers and strange objects at him, seeking priceless advice.

Needle shuffled his way to the back of the queue. It was now or probably never. Time to *speak up*. His heart thumped, sweat bubbled on his forehead. *Do it*, his toes told him as they scratched against the pebbles in his boots. He counted to ten, over and over. Was the room really swaying?

DING! DING! The sound of Lord Buckram hitting his glass with a spoon filled Needle's head with spikes of silver and, before he knew it, he was back standing at his post beside the cake.

"Ladies and Gentlemen! May I have your attention?" Lord Buckram was leaning over the table, facing Master Sharp. When the last of the laughs and coughs faded, he continued. "Dear Master Sharp. If you would spare me a minute of your time…" He adjusted a long bundle under his arm and awaited a response. "Ahem, Master Sharp?"

Master Sharp patted the shoulder of the man he was advising and turned to look at Lord Buckram. "Forgive me!" He raised his hands in a warm welcome. "Yes, dear friend? Time for cake?"

Lord Buckram smiled proudly and raised a hand to his heart. "Master Sharp, I had planned on doing this *after* your presentation; however, with the slight delay in proceedings, I thought there is no time like the present." He looked at Master Sharp, seeking approval to continue.

Master Sharp glanced at the cake and licked his lips. He possibly sighed, Needle was not sure, but then he smiled at Lord Buckram to continue.

"On hearing of your plans to come to Inthington, my team and I were most honoured to host this evening. Fitzroy's Master Chef gathered ingredients from afar, our finest wine was selected, my gallery's Hall of Great Masters transformed into a room befitting such a spectacular occasion…" The audience clapped their approval.

"But to demonstrate our true appreciation we present you with a gift. A gift created, *invented*, if you will, by Inthington's most spectacular Master Craftsman of all, especially for you – you being a Master of *your* fine craft." Lord Buckram laid the yellow silk-wrapped walking cane on the table before him. "For you, Master Sharp…"

The room was quiet but for the sound of shifting

chairs, flapping beads and creaking bodices as necks were stretched high in an attempt to see the gift, annoyingly obscured by the five-tiered cake.

"Well I never. Thank you, Lord Buckram," said Master Sharp. He stood up and gave Lord Buckram's hand a vigorous shake. "So, what do we have here? Shall we take a look, Ladies and Gentlemen?" he roared to the crowd.

The guests clapped and cheered and several rose from their seats.

"Come, come!" cried Master Sharp as he beckoned all two hundred or more guests to rise from their seats and join him at the top table.

The space around the cake was soon teeming with guests and Needle was nudged and elbowed out to the side of the room. He squeezed his way along the tight gap between crowd and wall, wincing as he smudged the mural's wet paint. He paused to see if anyone had noticed before pulling himself up to sit on the deep sill of a window.

He could see Master Sharp. He was facing a heaving crowd waiting patiently for the burst of energy to settle. When stillness fell, Master Sharp pulled the two loose ends of the gold bow that secured the bundle and peeled back the corners of silk.

Master Sharp turned to the crowd before running his fingers along the length of the polished cane and whistled out a quiet breath. Needle witnessed his every move and could not help but smile; if only Glory could see this moment! *Her* moment! As Master Sharp used two flat palms to fish the cane out from the casing of yellow silk, Needle sucked in his lips and made a quiet sch-m-ock sound; the perfect sound to make when treasures were born.

Master Sharp held the cane high in his palms and studied its jewel-encrusted handle, mud treasure transformed, twisting it this way and that. He scanned the cane from left to right, moving from its ball-shaped handle, along the polished wood, all the way to its silver foot.

The reflected light bounced off the gems, dotting every surface like a glistening river in morning light.

"*Treasure*," announced Master Sharp. Needle clamped his eyes shut, wishing the golden sparkles that exploded in his mind would last a moment longer. Master Sharp turned and looked at Lord Buckram.

"Who, may I ask, is this great Master Craftsman? I simply *must* shake their hand."

"I expected you would, Master Sharp," replied Lord Buckram with a grin. "In fact, she's here with us tonight."

"One moment, coming through!" came a spikey voice from deep within the audience.

A wave of grumbles travelled through the crowd as Mrs Quick trampled on silk shoes and prodded her way to the front where she straightened the headband wire that held up her one remaining black silk butterfly. She grabbed a handful of her dress in each hand and offered a wobbling curtsey.

On sight of her, Lord Buckram tutted and turned to face the yellow curtain. "Don't be shy, little one – come," he said. Much like before, when Lord Buckram visited the Frippery & Fandangle Emporium, he saw Glory's wooden finger curling around the curtain.

"Master Sharp, Ladies and Gentlemen, meet our Master Craftsman: Miss Gloria Bobbin."

Chapter Twenty-three

"I know quality when I see it," confirmed Lord Buckram over the cheers of the audience.

"PERFECTION!" added Master Sharp. He congratulated Glory with the longest handshake Needle had ever seen, before holding his walking cane before him for all to see. "Young lady, real talent *always* rises to the top."

"That it does," agreed Lord Buckram as he flashed a look over his shoulder at Mrs Quick, "no matter *who* or *what* velvet curtain is in the way." He winked at Glory – a wink that clearly said he knew any talent Mrs Quick claimed to possess was kept firmly hidden behind the curtain in the emporium.

Needle felt himself shine on Glory's behalf. He

looked around the room to see a sea of heads nodding their approval in her direction.

Lord Buckram turned to the crowd and raised his glass high. "A toast, Ladies and Gentlemen: to Gloria!"

The timing was perfect – Glory had the full attention of Master Sharp and the eyes of every person in the room. "Come on, Glory, *now*," Needle muttered to the backs of several spectators.

"TO GLORIA!" roared the crowd. Master Sharp reached over and clinked Lord Buckram's glass. It smashed and tinkled across the floor.

Glory yelped and snapped out of her rare moment of praise. "Another sign of death..." she cried, "when someone toasts you and glasses break." Her eyes searched the crowd. Needle bobbed up and down on the sill as best he could until she caught sight of him. He encouraged her with a nod.

Glory turned to face Master Sharp but suddenly there were people in her way.

"Oi! Watch it!" snapped Glory. A familiar peacock headband was waving inches from her nose. It blocked her view. Its wearer, doused in what must have been several bottles of expensive perfume, raised her head and kissed the air either side of Glory's face. Glory coughed her away.

The lady came at her again. "GLORIA, my dear friend! It's one of yours, isn't it?" Nodding wildly, she pointed at her headband until she was shoved to one side by another lady, larger this time, and dripping in more Frippery & Fandangle jewels than the shop window itself.

"These are *all* your designs, too, aren't they, Gloria darling?" Without waiting for confirmation, she yelled to the crowd that her jewels were *Gloria Bobbin Originals*, and flicked a dismissive hand towards Mrs Quick. Within seconds, Glory was surrounded, Mrs Quick was nowhere to be seen and Master Sharp was edging further and further away.

Needle cupped his hands over his eyes and peered out the window. It looked out at ground level and he could see the legs of the policeman guarding the room from outside. Through the relentless rain, he spotted a heaving wave of water breaching the foreshore wall. In the distance, several people were gathering at the corner of Eyelet Bridge and Broidery Quay. A man stood high on the plinth, pointing at the rising water.

"WHOA!" On the other side of the glass, a drenched Magpie flew from somewhere above and flapped her wings aggressively at the policeman. As the man leapt away, the tips of Magpie's feathers swept across the window before Needle; back and forth, back and forth.

Needle jumped down off the sill. The tide was turning! A sea-load of water was going to come charging up the raging river! He pushed through the bustling crowd until he reached the swarm that surrounded Glory as though she were a queen bee. "GLORY! THE TIDE! IT BE TURNING!" He ducked low. Like pulling a delicate clay pipe from the foreshore, he reached in with his arm until he had a good grip. He tried to wiggle her free.

"I CAN'T MOVE. TELL MASTER SHARP! NOW!"

Master Sharp was only feet away but, with the tangle of people between them, it felt like a mile. Manners wouldn't work. Needle pushed hard against the crowd. He caught a glimpse of his target and powered through, only to be bounced back and handed two empty glasses. He was being tossed and swirled by the crowd as though the flood had already hit. Master Sharp was edging further and further away, in the direction of the cake, with a determined look in his eye.

Needle gave one last push, and failed.

Master Sharp reached for the cake, plucked a sugared-lemon butterfly and popped it into his mouth. He sucked in his cheeks and flapped his elbows. The cake, Needle guessed, was good.

There was a SHRIEK! Needle shook the orange from his mind, but not before it burst into a joyous yellow. Another yellow shriek, and another! As though a stone had been dropped into water, the crowd rushed away from the cake like a tidal wave.

Needle blinked hard.

The cake! *It moved!*

Thousands of butterflies that cascaded down its side flickered and fluttered. They detached from the cake in one swirling solid shape and began to dance, so beautifully, around it.

"DEE-DEE!" cried Glory.

Needle dropped his two glasses. "DEE-DEE?"

Covered from head to toe in sparkling lemon butterflies, Dee-Dee roared, "GET TO MASTER

SHARP! WARN HIM! WARN HIM NOW!" She pulled the mesmerised crowd, like a powerful magnet, away from the cake and farther away from Master Sharp.

Master Sharp stood before Needle with nobody in between.

Needle's boots were glued to the floor. The man's face, all wrinkled with time and all those years of thinking important things, stared back. One bushy grey eyebrow hung low, just like Granda's back home. The other arched high and had been fiddled with and twisted into a sharp point.

Master Sharp leaned forward.

"You have something to say? To *warn* me, she said?"

Needle opened his mouth, his lips moved and the words, so many and so important, swirled around his head, but they never made a sound. Whatever way he jumbled them about, they were *unbelievable* words. His mouth was dry and he looked down at his trembling legs.

Glory elbowed him. "Tell Master Sharp your story, Needle, even if it makes you shake." She cocked her chin in the air. "You can do it. Promise." She crossed her heart.

Needle placed one hand in the crook of his back, raised his chin and stuck out his chest.

Master Sharp stood back and gave him some space. "That's better. Now tell me your story."

Chapter Twenty-four

"LADIES, GENTLEMEN, EVERYONE." Master Sharp's voice sliced through the crowd. "YOUR ATTENTION, PLEASE!"

The guests stopped chewing their sugared-lemon butterflies and turned.

From afar, Dee-Dee gave Needle a thumbs up and she collapsed into a chair. "PHEW!" she cried, and plucked the last of the sticky butterflies from her arms. Lord Buckram, still clapping in her direction, never looked so pleased.

Standing in Master Sharp's shadow, Needle gulped. The crowd rushed towards them until the top table's candlesticks and half-filled crystal glasses wobbled and the curtain beyond it swayed.

"THE TIME HAS COME! I now have *everything*

I need to demonstrate my invention!" Master Sharp placed a hand on Needle's shoulder. "Ready, young man?"

"Ready."

On Master Sharp's signal, Glory ran to the curtain and pulled it wide.

Needle bounded onto the stage and stood behind the most handsome stand that he had ever seen. It was a proper podium, not unlike the stand his schoolmaster used, but it was built with more brass than wood and its height was lower than expected. On its top, a small circle of metal sat on a pole; a *microphone*, Master Sharp had explained only moments before. A spider-web of wires spread out from the podium's base and climbed the walls until they disappeared through the Hall of Great Masters' domed ceiling.

Glory ran to Needle's side and angled the microphone close to his mouth. "Master Sharp was right, Needle – it's *your* story to tell." She poked him between his eyes. "No one can do it like you. Not even him!" There was so much smooth ivory pride to her words, Needle scrunched up his eyes. When he opened them again, she was gone. He faced the crowd.

The sound of his racing breath rushed around the hall like a winter's gale.

He stared back at hundreds of curious eyes.

Then stood straighter.

"I have a story…"

He jumped back several feet. A split second from when he'd spoken, his voice had thundered through the hall. It was huge! *Powerful!* Did it come from a giant? Or from him? Each word was crisp, so perfect, and *loud*. He came forward and watched as, like him, several spectators uncovered their ears. Eyes were wide open and breaths were held, waiting.

"It be a true story."

And so he began. His voice grew stronger, *braver*, so much so that Glory trembled with awe until Dee-Dee ran to her side and pulled her into a tight hug. Glory could picture his words as they flew through the crowd; words so true and so honest that, if they had a colour, she knew they would be white – the brightest, purest white she ever did see.

Like snakes of blinding, twisting light, his words crashed through the hall and climbed Master Sharp's wires, until they burst out onto the very roof of the gallery itself. In a flash, his warning was being blasted by Master Sharp's great invention, the likes of which no one had ever seen: an army of two hundred cone-shaped speakers that surrounded the gallery's great roof statue that pierced the clouds above.

As bright and quick as lightning, Needle's white rush of words cut through the air, drowning out the black roar of the River Notion with ease. His warning powered down the streets of Inthington Town, down its narrow lanes and down into the bedrooms of the oldest basement flats. Glory closed her eyes. She could see Needle's words catching the ear and turning the head of the river's planned first victim, Florence, as she laid her little sister down to sleep.

Satisfied, Needle's voice powered on and on.

Their message was being delivered.

Needle opened his eyes.

Silence.

He held his breath and stared back, and they accepted his stare. It was half a minute, he'd counted, before a thin voice came from deep within the crowd. "The snow, upriver... all that snow." Several heads turned.

It was followed by whispers.

"And the rain that followed. The river! Never been so high."

Needle heard a few gasps, some shuffling.

Like an itch that needed to be scratched, someone answered back, "But the river's walls are higher... much higher." There was a pause. "Aren't they?" The woman's voice was clearly laced in orange.

Everyone turned to face Needle again.

Lord Buckram marched up to him, wide-eyed. "There are reports of a major storm out to sea this evening. Some of my deliveries were cancelled because of it."

Master Sharp spoke urgently, "That will bring a surge of water into the river. And as for those dredging boats – clawing up the riverbed, making it deeper..."

Needle nodded. "I seen them schmocking boats! The more room they make, the more seawater will come to fill it. Then it will come over the wall."

"Could this really happen?" Lord Buckram asked and walked back and forth between Needle and Master Sharp. "*Could it?*" he squealed at Needle, filling Needle's mind with a shower of bright orange daggers. "This gallery is yards from the river. In all my years I never thought my priceless art would be at risk! At risk of *drowning*! This can't be right." He stared at Needle. "WHEN?"

All heads turned sharply to their left as a crashing sound filled the hall.

"MAGPIE!" cried Glory. She blinked her eyes tight with every loud bash of Magpie's wings against the window's glass, leaving behind splatters of desperate blood.

Needle ran to the window and placed his palms flat against its surface, willing his friend to stop. Magpie was warning them and her message was clear. Distant screams and muffled roars penetrated the glass from outside. Seconds later, black water, a foot deep, smacked against the window panes with force.

Needle turned to the crowd. "THE FLOOD! IT BE HAPPENING, NOW! EVERYONE! Forget your things. Go to what matters – your loved ones. Carry them to safety – as far as you can go. GO!"

"THIS WAY! THIS WAY!" Lord Buckram stood high on a table directing the crowd away from the flooded side entrance and towards a stairway

that led to the foyer. As though the hall was tilted, chairs fell and tables lurched as the crowd poured out.

"YOU! BOY!" Officer Pocket grabbed Needle by his collar and spun him around. He towered over him. "You said fourteen names…?"

Glory pulled at her uniform to find her bag. "We've a list, Officer Pocket – from the shards." She used her lips and her hand to unfold the damp page. "We think the unnamed prisoner is Needle's papa."

Dee-Dee stood in front of Officer Pocket, hands on hips. "That's the 'Sharp Thief' to you. You heard

275

Needle's story – his father is *not* a thief." She glared at him until he nodded.

Glory handed over the list. "And the fourteenth name is missing… that's… that's me."

Needle grabbed her hand. Dee-Dee put an arm around her shoulder. Master Sharp, gloves already on, pointed his cane towards the door. "We need to get you home, Miss Glory."

Glory squirmed out of their hold and slapped Needle's hand. "I can look after myself— besides, it's your papa that needs our help."

"YOU GOTTA GO HOME, GLORY!" yelled Needle. "I can get Da myself. Tell her, Dee-Dee!"

Dee-Dee rolled her eyes. "Tell *her*? Seriously?"

Standing on her tiptoes, Glory saw Officer Pocket's helmet climbing the stairs. "He should be more careful, so he should…" She pulled something from her apron's pocket, threw it in the air and caught it again. With a wink, she lied, "Oops. Officer Pocket must have dropped his jail keys."

Master Sharp laughed from way down deep in his belly. "Fine work, Glory!" But his yellow tone suddenly changed. "I will find refuge upstairs, but GO! All of you! Go save Needle's father. Needle, get home, quick as you can. I have my doubts the bridge will even survive." His voice dropped to little more than a whisper, "Get to the hag stone before it's too late."

"Hag stone?" asked Dee-Dee. She didn't hear mention of it in Needle's speech.

"It's a stone," said Glory. "With a hole in it."

Needle made efforts to find his hag stone necklace between his shirt buttons.

"How the hell do you go through that tiny hole? I think you might be talking through your—"

"Not this hag stone. He be talking about the gap over the third arch on Eyelet Bridge – it be a giant hag stone. Da told me last night."

Glory checked, "Is that all you have to do, Needle? To go home? Go into the hag stone?"

"I needs to be holding treasure—"

Master Sharp raised his hand. "As I told Needle, this part of his story must be kept secret or goodness knows what might happen. Now, Needle, go save your father. Please, you *must* hurry."

Needle flashed a look at Master Sharp – his words had suddenly faded from gunmetal-grey to the deepest blue. But before Needle could even blink, his mind filled with spikey silver flashes. Just as it cleared, it happened again, and again. Four times in total.

He spun around. "THE WINDOWS!" Several more smashed, allowing a torrent of black water to gush into the hall and, with it, a desperate crow.

"MAGPIE!" Needle held out his arm but lost his balance when ice-cold water slammed into his legs.

Glory whistled so loud, Needle was blinded. "MAGPIE! TAKE THEM!" She threw the ring of jail keys high into the air just as she, too, lost balance. Magpie squawked, swooped around Master Sharp's head, and caught the keys.

"GET THEM TO DA!" Needle howled but the bird was already gone. He took off towards the stairway. Glory and Dee-Dee had reached it first.

Following the last of the crowd, they ran up the stairs. A white hot snap filled Needle's mind before everything around him went pitch black.

"THE LIGHTS!"

"MASTER SHARP?" Needle screamed into the darkness. He threw himself down the stairs, not caring for its steps. His ankles twisted, his knees scraped and elbows bashed, he rolled and rolled until he landed on his side, entirely submerged in freezing water. "MASTER SHARP!" he roared as soon as his lips felt the air, his voice barely audible against the blackness of the water's roar as it powered through the windows.

In complete darkness, he braced himself against a pillar and, against the raging force of thigh-high water, circled it. He opened his eyes so wide they hurt, searching for a hint of something to see, *anything*.

He held his breath – did a flash of orange fill his mind? Quicker than a finger-snap? Did he hear something without even knowing it?

"AGAIN! MASTER SHARP! SAY IT AGAIN!"

"Needle!"

This time he'd heard it. As he expected, and for no more than a second, his mind filled with orange. But, strangely, somehow through it, the pitch-black hall took shape. It was almost imperceptible, but it was there – a flicker of orange light had bounced off the water and bathed the painted walls. Like viewing it all from a raging sea, the painted scenes of rivers and mountains flashed alive around him. Before he could think, the black roar of the water filled his mind and all that was orange was suddenly drowned out.

"AGAIN! SAY IT AGAIN! DUNNO HOW, BUT I BE SEEING WHEN YOU SPEAK!"

"NEEDLE!" Master Sharp roared and roared.

Needle reached him. He grappled with Master Sharp's cane and ignored the shards of glass that stabbed at his legs. Through the rising water, he counted the steps back to the stairway and heaved Master Sharp up.

"I can't thank you enough," panted Master Sharp. "But you *must* go. Together, you can save your father and get home, I'm sure of it. And that was one clever crow…" The noise level rose as soon as they reached the grand foyer of the gallery. Master Sharp moved closer to Needle's ear. "Trust her with your life."

A line of light jumped its way towards them. "NEEDLE!" Glory's torchlight met with the gem-encrusted handle of Master Sharp's cane as he held it out before him. It sent out shots of light like tiny falling stars in the dark.

Chapter Twenty-five

Needle whistled and whistled for his crow.

"MOVE IT!" screamed Glory from the bottom of the gallery's twenty steps. "WE NEED TO GET TO THE JAIL BEFORE IT'S TOO... AAGH!" Master Sharp had insisted she borrow his new cane but, even with its help, she struggled to stay on her feet in swells of ice-cold, thigh-high water.

Several steps up, Needle urgently scanned the scene before him for Magpie. His eyes bulged. Having dumped everything they had, the black clouds were parting. The cold moonlight fell on wave after wave heaving its weight over the embankment wall, each racing as fast as a panicked horse. Motorcars were tossed aside, debris thrashed and smashed together.

He whistled for Magpie one last time. Where *was*

she? Did she bring the keys to Da? Willing it to be true, he tried to picture her, swooping through the cell window, dropping keys into his hand. "OH NO! SHE BE TOO LATE!" He turned and looked at Dee-Dee, terror in his eyes. "Da's window. It be under water by now." He grabbed her arm and they charged down the steps.

Before Needle reached it, Dee-Dee had stormed into the water but her legs were swept from under her. Glad of the extra weight of pebbles in his boots, Needle jumped in and stood firm as a swell smashed into him.

He helped her up. Dee-Dee yelled and kicked at the water in rage. She grabbed Master Sharp's cane from Glory. "TAKE THE OTHER END!" She poked its silver foot at Needle and ordered her sister to stand between them, with the cane supporting her back.

Together they fought back until a ferocious wave crashed into, and took with it, the embankment wall. Its boom was deafening. Like a planned attack, it pushed the water stronger and faster in their direction. With a surge of strength, they lunged towards the first trunk in a row of trees. Holding on tight, they

screamed as the torrent raced down Ribbon Lane towards several police officers, led by Officer Pocket. They were banging on flooded basement doors, pulling children wrapped in bed sheets and terrified parents up onto the street.

Glory gasped. "LOOK!" She pointed to a man in the middle of it all – Landlord Hempenstall; not helping but pulling at his ratty hair and howling like a wolf at his water-damaged houses. "OI! YOU!" Glory took a deep breath to yell something red but Needle turned her head towards Eyelet Bridge.

"WE NEED TO CROSS THE BRIDGE. FAST!"

"WHOA!" she cried. The bridge curved high at its middle, but on either end mighty old blocks, too heavy for any man to bear, were being pushed like bales of hay across the road. On its nearest corner, a torrent of water swirled and charged around the statue-less plinth.

She turned to face Needle. Her eyes were stamped with fear but they told him, loud and clear: KEEP GOING. Using lampposts and tree trunks, they edged their way closer and closer to Eyelet Bridge.

They heaved themselves up onto the bottom block of Master Sharp's plinth where water swirled ankle-deep. Needle climbed higher and looked across the river towards Inthington jail, only visible in snatches where its walls blocked out the stars between the clouds. His eye followed the line of the river until he saw one pale dot – a face, the only one racing towards the bridge, not away.

"Da? DA?" Needle waved his arms frantically. Wings swooped down and smacked his head. "MAGPIE? MAGPIE! IT'S DA! IT'S DA!"

Dee-Dee faced the other way, studying her road home. "GLORIA. TIME TO GO."

From one block down, Glory tugged at Needle's trouser leg and yelled over the river's roar. "GO, NEEDLE! GET YOUR PAPA AND GO HOME!" Though her voice was strong, it was so icy blue, he crumbled to his knees. Leaning down, he thumb-wiped the tears that rolled down her face and smudged his own away, too.

She gulped, "Get home safely, DO YOU HEAR? You'll come back someday, won't you? Through this hag stone of yours?"

Needle urgently looked towards the third arch of the bridge. The ground beneath them trembled. "Dunno," he said, but this time – knowing the hag stone might not survive – he meant it. He shouted as loud as he could, "I WON'T BE FORGETTING YOU, GLORY."

"Well, let's make sure of that." She yanked her pouch bag open with her teeth and pulled out her green ragdoll. She kissed it, pushed it back in and stuffed the bag into Needle's pocket. "TAKE IT! Every time you listen to Doll's story, you'll see what she means to me; she knows my biggest secrets, and that's why I want you to have it. Please don't forget me."

Dee-Dee put her arm around Glory.

"*WHAT?* So I'm twelve and I have a doll..." said Glory, shamelessly; there was no point being embarrassed about it now.

Needle's voice cracked as he spoke, "Soon as I get home I be making something for you – the nicest thing I ever did make, and I'll get it to you. One way or the other." He looked up into the black sky where Magpie swirled in anxious tight circles.

"And don't forget this, Needle..." Shivering uncontrollably, Glory swung her arm around her back and lifted her chin high. "You can *always* do it."

"*We* can."

Glory looked up and smiled. "Bye-bye, Nee..." Her voice broke.

Dee-Dee planted a big-sister kiss on Needle's forehead and jumped back into the raging water. Bracing herself against the torrent, she helped Glory down.

Glory never once took her eyes off Needle.

"WAIT!" Needle jumped in, waded towards her and, despite the icy coldness of his touch, gave her the warmest of hugs.

Chapter Twenty-six

At the far end of the bridge, Needle peeled his father's hand away from a lamppost he'd clung onto. He wrapped one end of his rope belt around his father's trembling fist and the other around his own. "DON'T LET GO!"

"USE THE PARAPET, NEEDLE! THE WALL!"

Needle kicked his legs until his boots met with the drowned wall that ran the full length of the bridge. Needle clawed at the parapet's blocks until he heaved himself and his father out of the furious, waist-deep water and up onto the highest point of the bridge.

They stood, panting, above Eyelet Bridge's third arch.

The ground trembled. Another warning.

Needle leaned over the parapet wall and stared

down into the violent river as it powered towards them. He gasped. The river bulged like a breathing giant, the bridge's arches swallowed whole beneath its surface. He pointed down to the thick wooden plank that jutted out from the face of the bridge. Hiding below it was the hag stone gap.

"THE JOIST, DA! THERE!"

His father nodded. What they were about to do was packed with danger, they both knew it, but they also knew what prize lay beyond: the only place they could call home.

Without words, they climbed over the parapet wall and jumped down onto the joist. Needle sat down, straddling his legs either side of it. Flattening his back against the trembling blocks of the bridge, he peered down. The river was only inches from the hag stone gap and, with each heave, it spilled water with force through the gap and into the empty chamber.

"FEET FIRST," he yelled into his father's ear. He cupped his hands over his father's fist. "HOLD ON TIGHT. *TIGHTER*." For added support, Needle hooked his lower legs together beneath the joist. "GO!" he cried.

His father twisted his body and dropped over the

side, grabbing the joist with one arm. He swung his legs out of the water and towards the hag stone gap. On the third swing, his heels reached it. He released his arm and hung from the belt as his ripped heels felt for the way forward. Just as the skin on Needle's hands began to split against the force of the belt, Needle's father edged his body into the hag stone.

"NEEDLE!" he yelled.

Needle was standing on the joist, belt still wrapped around his bleeding fist. Through the darkness, he was staring at Magpie; she was flying up high, then diving low at the corner where the bridge met Broidery Quay. People were standing on the plinth, staring into the water. Next to them, someone waded desperately towards the river.

"GLORY!"

There was determination in her eyes. Needle looked down into the river. By the light of the lamps that flickered above the embankment wall, he saw bony fingers with blood-red nails clinging to the blocks beyond the first arch. A pale face surfaced, gasping for air, before disappearing below the black water.

"Mrs Quick, Da! It be Mrs Quick... Glory's mistress!"

"It's no good, Needle. You can't help," Needle's father spluttered as another wave of water splashed into the gap. "You need to jump, NOW!"

Needle looked at Glory. She was now at the river's edge, her legs butting up against what was left of the crumbling embankment wall. Dee-Dee was pulling at her arm, failing to drag her back.

"SWIM TO ME, MRS QUICK!" Glory screamed until her voice cracked. "DO IT, I'LL CATCH YOU!" She beckoned with her wooden hand.

Mrs Quick's eyes were wild with fear. She shook her head, swallowing mouthfuls of water. As she spluttered and coughed her head ducked, again, below the surface.

"MRS QUICK! SWIM! DO IT!" cried Glory.

Needle pulled fistfuls of his hair as he watched Glory climb over the embankment wall. She pushed herself into the full wrath of the river. Dee-Dee leaned dangerously over the wall, clinging to her sister's dress.

"NOW, NEEDLE!" screamed his father, "OR NEVER!" A wave forced him to retreat further into the gap. He was gasping for air.

Needle looked at Glory, then his father. How could

he choose just one to help? Like the plaque that held both their names, his heart was being ripped apart.

The shards were right all along.

There was a wild roar from the plinth. It was Rosie Selvage – the blond, necklace-stealing, pebble-throwing girl. Her brother Marcus stood, white-faced, several blocks up. Rosie, with her one bit of good, grabbed the hands of her two pickpocket friends and charged towards Dee-Dee. Together, they formed a human chain and Glory edged closer and closer to Mrs Quick.

She was only an arm's length away.

"HELP THEM! HELP THEM!" Needle hollered at Marcus. The boy stared back blankly and didn't budge.

Magpie squawked. Needle looked down. Glory was gone.

"GLORRRRRRY!" he roared and roared until a cry of relief howled from his throat; bursting through the surface, Glory had pulled Master Sharp's cane from her clamped wooden fist, and reached Mrs Quick.

Needle swung from the joist and lunged towards the gap. He fell into the water and his full body smashed against the bridge. His father heaved with all his might until, head first, Needle squirmed his way in.

It was pitch dark in the chamber. Blind and standing in knee-high, stone-cold water, Needle's legs throbbed. His feet had lost all feeling, except for the beat of the raging river as it drummed the walls and made the rock itself shake.

Magpie flapped and squawked between them, dipping down to the water's surface.

"Not now, Magpie," warned Needle's father.

"I think she be trying to tell us someth—"

"Hand me my box of treasures," ordered his father. "Do it quick, Needle, we need to hold the drawer handle from home before it's too late."

Letting go his father's hands, Needle reached for the strap of his satchel. "Oh no! Da! I don't have it – my satchel, I left it somewhere…"

Needle's father swiped Magpie away as she grappled for their attention and grabbed Needle's shoulders. "WHERE? Needle, think. We must get it! Holding treasure from 1928 was how we got here, so to leave we must do it again with a treasure from home. It's our only chance."

"I dunno, Da! Wait – the van! I left it there when

we found the uniforms." Needle scrambled for the wall and reached high for the gap. A waterfall now gushed over its edge and poured down on Needle's head. "You wait here, Da," he managed, "but help me – my foot, grab it and push me up." Needle raised his foot but, before his father could help him, Magpie pecked hard at his shin. "Get off, Magpie! Da, my foot!"

"Needle, there's no time for the drawer handle," said Needle's father. He reached down and slapped the rising water, gauging the speed at which it was rising. "We *both* need to get out of here." He grabbed Needle's foot and pushed him up.

Needle forced his head and shoulders into the gap. The river heaved and water rushed in. He tried to hold his head above the water but it was too late; the river filled the whole gap. He had to retreat.

Needle landed on his knees and struggled to stand. The water had risen beyond his hip. The full force of the river cascaded down into the chamber. Inch by inch, second by second, the water rose.

"On my shoulders, Needle, NOW!"

Needle clambered on to his father's shoulders and took a deep breath before pushing his head back into the gap. Once more, the force threw him back and he fell to the ground. As he surfaced, he was attacked; Magpie's wings slapped his arms. She twisted and pulled his hair. Aiming for the back of his neck, she pecked hard. Needle froze – Master Sharp's departing words echoed through his mind: *Trust her with your life.*

"WHAT IS IT?" Needle screeched before falling to the side. He grabbed at the floor and pushed his hands off it with all his might. The water was now chest high. His heart was gripped by fear: *they were going to drown.* He raised his arms high, flapping and flailing for his father.

As his father pulled him into the tightest of hugs, Needle felt Magpie's wings gently brush off his right arm. And there, in his own clenched fist, he felt something extraordinarily familiar.

He had picked up his very own handcrafted candlestick, assembled and etched for his mother in the safety of his trove only days ago, yet in a time that was sixty odd years before.

As the water rose higher, Needle lay his head on his father's chest and Magpie, standing on his shoulder, nestled her head against his cheek. A shock of icy cold hit his palm where the candlestick lay. He closed his eyes and whispered, "Let me tell you its story: Mam, poor Mam – she waited and searched and prayed for us each day, Da. She walked our foreshore as soon as the sun rose, under Eyelet Bridge and down as far as the jail – she even took off her shoes and squeezed her toes into the pebbles, not caring for who saw her. Each night, she would light a candle, place it in this candlestick and sit in your chair, Da. She knew I must have gone far, far away, searching for you. And when she searched some more and finally found your empty bag in the gap over the third arch, she left this candlestick right here, Da – *proper treasure*, for us. Happened sixty odd years ago, at least."

As the water finally rose too high, he felt it: her soft arms were wrapped around him, a blast of warm air with the smell of swirling turf smoke and something delicious in the pot. And all he could hear was the sound of her humming his favourite yellow tune.

They were home.

Chapter Twenty-seven

Like a thief, the cold January air slid into the cottage. Even before the old front door had ricocheted against its white-washed wall, the uninvited guest whipped around the room, scooping up swirls of turf smoke and stealing warm, home-scented air.

Mr Luckett had only made it one step in when he crumbled to his knees. Leaving his rocking chair still rocking beside the glowing stove, Needle's mother ran to embrace them, pressing their heads tight against her warm neck. On the backs of their own, they felt the heat of her hands giving three little squeezes: *I-love-you*. Speechless, she swayed and swayed, humming her favourite tune about home, sweet home.

Bursts of soft, primrose yellow filled Needle's

head, tickling his every thought with pure happiness. Pure *joy*.

Lifting Needle's chin, she looked deep into his eyes. She could see something new, of course, something different. But her growing smile and gentle nod told him it was something she had expected all along: *courage*.

She finally found her voice.

"My brave, brave boy. You brought home the most precious treasure of all."

Chapter Twenty-eight

It was early the following Monday morning when Glory approached Eyelet Bridge or, at least, what was left of it. Two of the five arches had collapsed, their blocks dragged for miles downriver towards the gaping mouth of the sea. Master Sharp stood high on the statue-less plinth, waving his pencil and drawings as he co-ordinated what appeared to be a well organised rebuild. His coat sleeves bunched high up his arms and his hair tossed in the wind but, even from that distance, Glory could see that his eyebrow was perfectly tweaked.

"GLORY! DEAR GLORY!" he shouted down to her when he saw her, standing hands on her hips in ankle-deep water. He quickly folded his drawings and wedged them under his arm. "We'll have our bridge sorted in no time!" Muttering something under his breath, he began to lower himself down the plinth. With one block to go, he turned and greeted her with the biggest, warmest smile.

Glory beamed. "Here's your cane, Master Sharp." She held it out, proudly. "And not a scratch wrong with it, you'll be glad to hear."

A gust of wind caught him and he wobbled a bit. "Perhaps it's high time I put it to good use, Glory! If you would be so kind as to pass it here."

"Sure, Master Sharp." Glory held it up to him, confident in the knowledge that it would easily bear the weight of any man.

Master Sharp wrapped his hand around the ball-shaped handle. In no more than a split second, the cane crashed to the ground.

Glory gasped. She'd seen it: as soon as Master Sharp touched the handle, he'd flinched. She looked up and witnessed him turn over his hand. There, in the centre of his palm – precisely where he had gripped the cane – rose a blister.

"The cane's shard!" cried Glory. "It burned you... but... how? It's only hot to Needle and his papa..."

"Ah!" said Master Sharp. He shook his head and

began to chuckle. "You've caught me!" He climbed down off the plinth and stood before her. His cheeks were definitely red.

She tilted her head and her brows dipped. Did Master Sharp just bob from one foot to the other? Just as her friend would do?

"N...N...Needle?" She shook the idea away. "NO WAY."

He nodded.

She folded her arms. "You're lying."

He winked, leaned forward and whispered in his best twelve-year-old voice: "Never told a lie in my life. Not one, Miss Glory!" He stared deep into her eyes.

Glory gulped. He'd sounded just like Needle! She tried to say something, even raised her wooden hand, but, for once, she found herself lost for words. The greatest inventor in all the world was her friend Needle?

It was too hard to believe!

But it was also *easy* to believe.

"You? *My* Needle?" she finally managed.

He smiled. "*Your* Needle. Promise." He crossed his heart on his heartless, right side.

Glory squealed and squealed – something he could

not quite make out, but whatever it was, it was joyous yellow. He laughed from way down deep in his belly until tears filled his eyes.

She stopped to catch her breath. "MY NEEDLE!" She poked his shoulder hard, as she would have often done. He stumbled a bit but she caught him and grimaced a quick apology.

"No apologies needed, Glory. I'm the same Needle up here, you know," he said as he patted the side of his head. "Though I have figured out quite a bit since then." She was surprised to see him blush as he continued, "I was quite the sharp thinker as a boy, if I say so myself, so, for years, they called me 'Needle-Sharp'. The 'Sharp' name stuck like glue. Of course, the 'Master' part came much later – with a little bit of success, perhaps."

Glory giggled, some of it escaping as a snort. "Just a bit, I'm sure," she said as she thought of his world-famous inventions.

Her mind began to swirl, and it wasn't missed.

"It came as a bit of a shock to me, too – even though I was expecting you. After twelve-year-old me travelled to 1928, I made it back home to 1864 and lived my full life, right up to this very moment." He laughed at some distant memory and said, "It took me a long time before I realised I was growing into that old man I'd saved in the flooded ballroom!"

Glory struggled with everything Master Sharp said and wondered how on earth Needle ever managed to become so full of complicated information. "So… so, Needle didn't know? He didn't know that you were… eh, *himself*," she frowned as she stumbled over her own words.

"No. And it was very important that twelve-year-old me did *not* know – goodness knows what devilment I'd have gotten myself into had I known!"

"MAGPIE!" cried Glory as a crow swooped low overhead. It landed several feet away, grabbed a drowned mouse and flew away.

Master Sharp shook his head, "Just an ordinary crow, I'm afraid."

"Will I ever see her again?"

Master Sharp folded his technical drawings into a long rectangle and pointed it towards the gaping hole where the chamber over the third arch once stood. "Give me time to repair the hag stone, and then we'll see."

Glory stepped closer to the remains of the parapet

wall and peered down. The hag stone had fallen into the river and the tip of its smooth hole jutted out of the water. Two lucky magpies stood squabbling on its top, but Glory failed to feel the joy.

"Oh! Without the hag stone we'll never see her! Will we?" She meant Needle too, of course, but felt shy about that when faced with the same, yet older, person.

"I can't tell," said Master Sharp with the cheekiest of grins. He tipped the side of his nose as though holding in a sneeze or perhaps a secret.

Glory huffed louder than she intended; did he mean *can't* tell or *won't*?

"A seat?" suggested Master Sharp. He patted the first block of the plinth and gave his drawings one further fold before laying them down as a dry seat for her. Glory sat well to the drawings' right and patted them gently for the old man to sit. She winked; he laughed.

"After twelve-year-old me had the pleasure of meeting you in 1928, my mind started ticking the second I set foot back in 1864. I was always curious, you see. I understood how we managed to travel – my father explained it well: read a treasure's story when through the hag stone." Glory nodded her understanding so he continued, "But I always wondered how the shards from 1928 arrived in 1864 in the first place. Treasure from the *future?*" He poked himself several times between his bushy eyebrows, "Tick, tick, tick, my mind was going. I decided to investigate the hag stone further and soon discovered Magpie's old nest."

He reached into the inside pocket of his coat and pulled out a small hessian pouch. It was frayed at the edges where brown string held it closed. He nodded at Glory to open her wooden hand and tipped out its contents.

Glory looked at the shiny silver coin in her palm. "It's lovely. *Five pence*, it says."

"Like a shilling. Turn it over, if you would. I can't touch it, it's hot." He patted his knees in anticipation.

Glory flashed a look at Master Sharp and quickly turned it over. "2028? This coin is from 2028?"

His voice rose with every word; "A world one hundred years into the future that you and I could hardly begin to imagine!" He jumped to his feet, adrenaline pumping through his old veins as he thought of all the inventions yet to be born. "A world

that is the real home to our dearest of friends –
Magpie!"

Glory shook her head. "I don't understand."

"Magpie is from the future. I found several coins
such as this in her nest, so I'm sure she didn't mind
me borrowing this one." He winked.

"So Magpie brought the shards to 1864?"

"So I believe. Seems she wasn't happy with
the future she found herself in, so she made it her
business to change that. I'm assuming time itself tore
that plaque to shreds, and when it did, she was able to
carry them in her beak."

Hooking her arm around his, Glory hugged his
shoulder. She returned the future coin to its pouch
and offered it back.

"Keep it. Practise with it and maybe, one day, you'll
feel its heat."

On hearing a toot from one of the 'schmocking'
boats, he rose to his feet. "Ah, it's time to raise the
hag stone. Shall I see you soon, Glory? We have your
emporium to consider, after all, and it must be good
enough for the Queen to visit, every single day! Oh,
one more thing," he said as he dug deep into his
pocket, "Now that you are in my life again, I won't

be needing this." He pulled out countless metal tools, several muddy treasures thrown up by the flood and, finally, a stringy green handful of material.

"Doll!" cried Glory.

Master Sharp leaned across and wiped away a tear that dropped from her lashes onto her cheek. "A happy one, I'm guessing?" He pulled his pencil from his ear and went back to his business.

Chapter Twenty-nine

The clocktower chimed nine when Glory reached the doorless front entrance of the Frippery & Fandangle Emporium. It was flooded, of course, with collapsed glass cabinets floating much like coffins across the floor. From the doorway, she saw snakes of coloured beads slowly rotating and dancing in the early morning light. The water was now only knee-deep, but it made its deeper presence known high up on the ruby velvet curtain. Glory waded over to it and, with every step, something once precious crunched under her heavy boots. When she reached the curtain, she held up her hand, keeping it level with the murky brown line that crossed the material. She carefully brought her hand back where it met her chin.

"Four foot deep, at least," she whispered.

"What time do you call this?" came a tired voice from behind the curtain.

Glory shrieked and covered her mouth with her hand. After a few nervous breaths, she slowly pulled the heavy curtain to one side.

"Mrs Quick," she managed. "Good morning."

Mrs Quick and a bedraggled looking Maximus were sitting on the workshop's only piece of furniture that appeared to remain intact: Glory's strong desk with its iron legs and thick wooden top. Mrs Quick was wrapped in an unremarkable, floor-length navy coat, the bottom of which sank deep into the water. She wore a plain black cloche hat, strangely void of any fancy beadwork or feathers and had it pulled so far down her pale face that her eyes were hidden. She remained silent, and Glory took this as an instruction to explain herself.

"Sorry I'm late, Mrs Quick," she began. Mrs Quick didn't even flinch so Glory felt the need to continue. "The roads, well, they were blocked as I'm sure you know, and by the time I got to Eyelet Bridge – they were right what they were saying – it's all but gone!"

Mrs Quick made a short huffing sound in reply. "Mrs Quick, I *said* I'm sorry."

"I have been waiting for you to…"

Glory could feel her cheeks redden so fast as only Mrs Quick could cause. "Oh, for goodness' sake, Mrs Quick – I'm what? *One hour* late. You should be thanking your lucky stars I… *we* got here at all… or have you forgotten how I jumped into that freezing water to get to you?"

Mrs Quick pushed herself off the desk and took one step towards Glory.

"AH, do you know what, Mrs Quick? You can go and—"

"ENOUGH, child. There is the important matter of the future of this establishment to consider."

Glory looked up at her tight lips and felt ready to finally put this woman and her ridiculous priorities in their rightful place.

Mrs Quick slowly removed her hat and placed it on Glory's desk. When she turned back to face Glory, something was amiss; yes, her angry mouth was as tight and scarlet red as ever, her pale skin stretched over her bony cheeks, black whiskers overdue a good plucking sprang out from her sharp chin. All normal.

But it was her eyes – they were, much to Glory's surprise, *smiling*.

"Gloria Bobbin. You – and no doubt the rest of this gossip-hungry town – have heard how my reputation... dare I say it... was *questioned* by Lord Buckram." She reached for Glory's wooden hand. Glory pulled it back, but Mrs Quick took it gently and sandwiched it between her gloved hands. "Gloria, we have a lot in common."

Glory raised her eyebrows; she struggled to agree.

"You are brave. *Brazen* almost. And full of fiery ambition. You see what you want and you make it happen, regardless of your... your *shortcomings*."

Glory tugged her hand back a little, instinctively wanting to punch back – she could list a few shortcomings in the woman before her with ease. But Mrs Quick held on tight and almost lovingly rubbed the smooth surface of Glory's wooden hand.

"But I fear you have something I will *never* have. You have the ability to put others *before* your ambition and, well, now I can see that strategy works in one's favour. Had I known, perhaps my reputation in this town wouldn't be in the gutter." The smile disappeared from Mrs Quick's eyes, "And rightly so, I suppose."

"Um, sorry about that," offered Glory. But this time she wasn't sorry for something she'd done or said in haste; she was sorry that Mrs Quick, who was strangely softening before her eyes, had always felt it necessary to be so unkind, so cruel, so mean. And sorry for whatever it was that had turned her into the hard woman she had become, as hard as wood itself.

"I *know* I have a... shall we say... less than kind reputation," confessed Mrs Quick, "so there's no need to mollify me, Gloria. I am well aware of *my* shortcomings. And for that, I *am* ashamed. And that is why I must leave."

She raised her hands up high and turned in a slow, wobbly circle. She took a deep breath and stopped when, once again, she faced Glory. "Take it, Gloria Bobbin – this emporium – take it all, and make it yours. Make it *spectacular*." She pulled her hat as far down on her head as it would go, tucked her stiff dog under her armpit and, fifteen steps later, departed the Frippery & Fandangle Emporium for the last time.

Glory stood in the middle of the shop floor. A swirl of water spun around her and the floating beads and feathers that had lined up at the walls joined the dancing water and sparkled their way around her skirt. She picked up a peacock feather and lay it across her wooden hand.

"Mine?" she asked it. She plucked random beads – two turquoise, one yellow – and cupped them in the palm of her hand. "All mine?"

Ever so gently, she tipped her hand back and forth and watched the beads cling to each other as they danced in her palm. They were now homeless, much like the many thousands of people in Inthington; although countless homes were destroyed, bridges had collapsed and several fine buildings, the Millbank Gallery included, would take years to recover, lives had been saved. And, much to her delight, Master Sharp was already making plans to ensure this town would thrive once again.

Glory sighed and whispered to the beads, "Start somewhere." She returned to her workshop and waded out to the corridor that led to the back door. Standing before the rows and rows of mahogany drawers that lined the wall, she ran her finger along the hand-scripted labels, found the turquoise beads' home and searched high for the drawer labelled 'yellow'.

"There you are," she said to the drawer that was just within reach. She dropped the yellow bead into its home and, as she pushed it closed, the drawer to its right caught her eye.

"*1864*," she read. The letters were void of any fancy swirls or serifs – they were blocky and bold, almost etched into the surface. She slid the drawer open. Standing high on her tiptoes, she reached in and folded her fingers around a package.

It was wrapped in white paper and was tied with a beautiful yellow ribbon.

Taking care not to drop it, she briskly returned to her desk and laid it on the damp surface. Noticing its fine layer of dust that sparkled in the morning light, she blew it gently and smiled. "The dust has finally settled," she whispered to her ragdoll, stuffed feet-first up her sleeve.

A piece of parchment paper stuck out from the ribbon at an odd angle. She carefully slipped it out, taking care not to tear its delicate corners, and turned it over.

Dear Glory,

Do you like my gift? I done it ages ago but it be takin me longer to lern writing. Did you no the shop key you left in your bag still werks in 1864? I be leaving your gift and this letter there tonite in one of them drawers up high so I hopes it will be there in 1928. I wont be touching nothing else in the shop, cross my heart.

Your friend,
Needle.

Spinning the package slowly until the perfect bow faced her, she placed it in the palm of her hand and paused to admire it.

She closed her eyes.

She could picture Needle, clear as day, in her mind – he was back in his trove, tinkering away, thinking no doubt of his journey to 1928. She smiled as she saw his kind eyes, his ragged clothes and muddy boots.

But one thing had changed and she could see that in his smile – he was *courageous*. So courageous he learned to write and so courageous he used the key from her pouch bag to place her gift in a drawer in the emporium back in 1864. And there it would stay, patiently waiting, until this very moment.

Taking a deep breath, she pulled the ribbon and opened her gift.

Tears rolled down her cheeks and she crossed her heart with her wooden finger. "It's perfect. Promise."

She ran her finger along her new silver hand. Much like her embroidered curtain at home, it was etched, like fine lace, with the tiniest trees and birds, dainty figures and playful animals, minuscule shoes and fancy hats. It was a thing of beauty, adorned with sea-glass and river-swept gems from another world, another time. And it was complete with discreet pearl buttons that, when pressed, released the tiniest of hidden tools – tools that would please the heart of any serious jeweller.

She turned it over and released the gentle grip of its four fingers to reveal a hag stone, a patient reminder with its perfectly carved hole, sitting in its palm.

Glory smiled. Having everything she would ever

need to run an emporium all of her own, and now knowing that her brave friend was living his life, she closed her eyes, put her wooden hand at the crook of her back and cocked her chin high. "It's *treasure*. Made sixty odd years ago, at least," she said. "Fine work, Needle."

THE END

The Truth be Known

– *The Great Flood of London, 1928* –

It is not unusual for a writer to be asked the question: *Where do your ideas come from? Elsetime* is fictional, of course – it's a make-believe story that took time to evolve and, as Needle would tell you, patience played a big part while I waited for sparks of inspiration to ignite. But, from the get-go, I had an imaginary cast of characters in my head, shouting *Pick me! Pick me!* There was Needle, a mudlark, who I instantly knew was from the 1800s. Then Glory and Mrs Quick, who told me they were from 1928. Encouraged by a gift-bearing crow that would visit my garden, Magpie joined in too. Much like how Needle would hold a treasure in his hand, I listened to their stories, waiting and wanting to hear more. Something BIG was about to happen in their world – I could feel it, perhaps in the beat of my heart.

Then I found treasure: a newspaper clipping from 1928 that told a true story: it reported that, on the night of the 6th January 1928, a flood tragically took the lives of fourteen souls along the River Thames in central London. It listed all of their names, including, much to my shock at the coincidence and sadness, that of a *Mrs Quick*. Although the events, characters and places in *Elsetime* are fictional, I had finally found inspiration and my story began. But now, as you hold this book in the palm of your hand, you might like to hear the *real*, true story of what happened that tragic night.

It was a recipe for disaster. The three ingredients: a white Christmas upriver, a brutal storm offshore, and man. Together, they brought us The Great Flood of London, 1928 – the last major flood to hit the city centre.

In the closing days of 1927, at the source of the River Thames, folk might have enjoyed a white Christmas, but a sudden thaw on New Year's Eve, followed by twice the normal fall of rain, doubled the volume of water that thundered down the Thames and out towards the sea. But that alone did not cause the water to breach the embankment walls. Another ingredient that brought suffering to so many, was the unfortunate timing of a storm in the North Sea. It coincided with a naturally high spring tide and it whipped up an enormous swell that rushed inland at the turn of the river's tide. It fought against the deluge of snowmelt and rain water, funnelling its way up the Thames, climbing higher and higher, faster and faster, helped greatly by the third ingredient: a grave mistake made by man. Over the course of several years, the river had been over-dredged to deepen a river channel for larger ships but this allowed the hungry sea more room, and, shortly after Big Ben's midnight chimes, time was up.

No doubt it was a spectacle to see majestic ships and small boats, untethered by the current, racing along the river high above street-level. But reality soon hit that long dark night when the water roared over the embankment walls. Outside the Tate Gallery (now the Tate Britain) in the Millbank, the wall, believed to have been part of an old prison, finally collapsed, slamming a river-load of water onto the streets. Within minutes, lives were being lost and buildings smashed with the power of several feet of water as it forced its way down into one-hundred-year-old basement flats, trapping London's most vulnerable before they hardly had time to realise their fate. In the blink of an eye, over four thousand people were homeless, Big Ben was surrounded, the Underground was submerged, the moat at the Tower of London filled for the first time in eighty years and the basement galleries at the Tate flooded.

Reports of heroic policemen and neighbours were abounded as they pulled barefoot children from basement flats, and dedicated staff at the Tate worked through the next day to salvage many fine works of art from their flooded galleries. Eighteen pieces were destroyed, hundreds more damaged, but miraculously, as some would say, the Whistler Murals – painted onto the walls of the gallery only weeks prior – survived despite being swamped in up to 8ft of water and mud. They can still be enjoyed today.

It took several years for the buildings of London to recover and a lifetime for others who lost loved ones.

The run-down slums were demolished and replaced by fine buildings, the walls repaired and heightened by a further few feet. But to finally put the fear of another flood to bed, proposals for a Thames Flood Barrier began with haste amongst inventors of the day. However, like the carving of a hag stone's hole, it took much determination and many, many years of patience until it was finally built in 1982.

To this day, other than markers showing how high the waters rose, no monument nor plaque is known to exist to commemorate the fourteen souls lost to the Great Flood of London, 1928.

Acknowledgements

HOORAY! Little did I know what it would take to write a book! Several years, for a start, and the support of amazing people along the way as I navigated this magical journey. It started with Alice, a fortune-teller who told me to Write! Write! Write!

I am immensely grateful to my treasure of an Agent, Josephine Hayes, to Jordan Lees and Amandeep for their support, and the team at The Blair Partnership. Thank you also to my publisher and editor, Mikka Haugaard, who made it all happen.

To my dear friends, Niamh Garvey, Olivia Hope, Colin McArdle, Ciara O'Connor, Fran Quinn, Aisling White, Susan and Kevin at the Big Smoke Writing Factory – superstars, one and all – only for you, my writing journey would have stopped short long ago. And to the wisest owl at the helm, Claire Hennessy, thank you for your awesome (no better word!) advice, your kindness and for holding my hand.

Each step of the way, I met precious gems who played a part in my journey: Vanessa Fox O'Loughlin for championing Elsetime from the get-go; Steve Voake for your encouragement at the Wells Festival of Literature; Jeremy de Quidt, my favourite human magpie, for your storytelling inspiration; Sarah Webb, what a role model; The junior judges and Caroline at the Bath Novel Award; Sinéad O'Hart and Adam Cannon for allowing me to bend your ear when the plot thickened too much for my liking. Thank you Laura Smythe for guiding me through that thing called PR. To Caroline, Elizabeth, Kieran, Marc, Muireann and Oran, thank you, writer friends both on-line and off, for helping me feel like I belong.

Huge love and huge thanks to my biggest fan, Dad (I did it!), dear Mum sprinkling good fortune from above, and to my favourite reader, Moira. To Rían (you rock!), and to Dee who, with each low this journey brought, kicked me straight back up to the high – thank you.

To Jerry, the apple of my eye, who patiently read every draft, redraft and half draft of Elsetime, hats off to you for putting up with it (and me!), I cannot put into words how truly grateful I am. And finally, to my fellow hag stone hunters, dearest Bobby and Faye – my *everything* and my whole world – I love you.

About the Author

Eve is a children's author and artist, living half way up a hill in Wexford, Ireland. With her hands already full with paintbrushes, twins, a stray cat and a dog, a mysterious fortune-teller once told her to pick up a pen and *Write! Write! Write!* She listened, and now, on the rare occasion where she's not scribbling a story, Eve enjoys painting everything from rather grown up pieces to children's murals.